Every writer has their own style and so does every artist. As children hardly any of us paid attention to the credits for the story would have commanded our whole attention. What stayed behind are the images, the art.

There have been many fine artists in *Tinkle* who left memorable, often impactful, visual impressions on my mind. But the one artist who touched my heart as a child and whose characters I found adorable—human or animal—was V.B. Halbe. His characters were endearingly rotund and displayed the quirkiest of expressions, aptly mirroring the bizarre situations they found themselves in. Ram Waeerkar's characters, to me, were distinctive and dynamic. You could imagine that one of them could come to life any moment, even in their comic avatar! Then there was Pradeep Sathe, who also went under the name Ajay Bana. When he drew an animal, bird, insect or flower, you could be sure it was as true to life as a photograph. These were the more frequently seen names in the early *Tinkle* magazines. The comic was also graced with the art of such stalwarts as Pratap Mullick, M. Mohandas, Souren Roy and K. Chandranath.

The writers made a mark on my consciousness only once I grew older and started relating the stories I liked with a particular style of writing. Of course the most favoured genre remains humour and I was no exception to this. I loved Anwar and his innocent wit—that was the hallmark of Subba Rao. Then there were Kalia the Crow's ingenious ways and the brilliant luck that always came to Shambu's aid, all products of Luis Fernandes' fertile imagination. Though different writers wrote Suppandi and Nasruddin Hodja, these two were particular favourites of mine, as they are among the many, many readers of *Tinkle*. And then, every child has a little bit of 'what if I didn't follow rules' edge to them. Through Tantri the Mantri and his adventures, the only beloved villain from the *Tinkle* stables, many of us got to indulge this side, even if vicariously.

Reading *Tinkle* brings back memories as much as it forms new ties to our child's hearts. As you flip through these pages, like me you too, I'm sure, will recall old favourites and make new connections that resonate with you. Here's to a joy to treasure—a joy that keeps on giving.

Happy reading,
Rajani Thindiath
Editor-in-Chief, *Tinkle*

"The content including the information, pictures, offers, contests and prizes is reproduced from the August 1983 to October 1983 editions of *Tinkle* No. 40 to 45 in its original and unaltered form to retain the essence of *Tinkle* Origins. Some of the facts may have been changed as of this day. Neither the offers nor prizes are currently valid. Any participation or claim in this regard shall not be entertained."

EDITOR-IN-CHIEF : **RAJANI THINDIATH**
GROUP ART DIRECTOR : **SAVIO MASCARENHAS**
EDITORIAL TEAM : **SEAN D'MELLO, APARNA SUNDARESAN,**
RITU MAHIMKAR, AASHLINE ROSE AVARACHAN,
JUBEL D'CRUZ, POOJA WAGHELA
HEAD OF CREATIVE SERVICES : **KURIAKOSE SAJU VAISIAN**
DESIGN TEAM : **TARUN SOMANATHAN, KETAN TONDWALKAR**
COVER DESIGN : **AKSHAY KHADILKAR**

© Amar Chitra Katha Pvt. Ltd., May 2019, Reprinted March 2020
ISBN 978-93-88957-00-7
Published by Amar Chitra Katha Pvt. Ltd., 7th Floor, AFL House, Lok Bharati Complex,
Marol Maroshi Road, Andheri (East), Mumbai – 400059, India
Tel: +91 22 4918 888 1/2
www.tinkle.in | www.amarchitrakatha.com
Printed in India

Get in touch with us:

✉ tinklemail@ack-media.com 🌐 www.tinkleonline.com
🐦 @TinkleMagazine 🌐 www.amarchitrakatha.com
f Tinkle Comics Studio 🌐 www.tinkle.in
📷 @tinklecomicsstudio 📮 Amar Chitra Katha Pvt.Ltd, 7th floor, AFL House, Lok Bharati Complex, Marol Maroshi Road, Andheri (East), Mumbai 400059

© Amar Chitra Katha Pvt. Ltd.
This book is sold subject to the condition that the publication may not be reproduced, stored in a retrieval system (including but not limited to computers, disks, external drives, electronic or digital devices, e-readers, websites), or transmitted in any form or by any means (including but not limited to cyclostyling, photocopying, docutech or other reprographic reproductions, mechanical, recording, electronic, digital versions) without the prior written permission of the publisher, nor be otherwise circulated in any form of binding or cover other than that in which it is published and without a similar condition being imposed on the subsequent purchaser.

INDEX

The Bird's Song	3
Nambi and His Protruding Stomach	11
Tinkle Tricks & Treats	13
Make Your Own Japanese Garden	14
Editor's Choice	15
See and Smile	17
Meet the Praying Mantis	18
The Fee	21
The Moon- Our Strange Neighbour- 2	23
Kalia the Crow	26
Say Hello to Dilip Kadam	
Adventures of Kasperle	29
Speed	35
Shikari Shambu	37
The Donkey and the Lion	40
Anwar	42
Mooshik	43
Did You Know?	44
Meet the Dolphin	46
The Day Jalebis Grew on Trees	50
Oh and Eh!	54
Meet the Golden Eagle	60
About See and Smile	
Nasruddin Hodja	65
Editor's Choice	67
Tinkle Tricks & Treats	69
Make Your Own Colourful Puppets	70
See and Smile	71
The Tiger, the Bear and the Man	72
The Boy and His Coins	75
The Moon- Our Strange Neighbour- 3	78

INDEX

The Face in the Window	81
Kalia the Crow	82
Stone Soup	85
The Clever Farmer	90
The Baby Elephant	92
Say Hello to K. Chandranath	
Meet the Spider	95
Anwar	99
Did You Know?	100
Editor's Choice	103
A Friend in Need	104
Searching for Sunken Treasure	106
Mooshik	109
The Dwarf Who Outwitted the Giant	110
Shikari Shambu	113
Sundar and the Seth	116
The King of Birds	124
Meet the Mule	127
Editor's Choice	130
Tinkle Tricks & Treats	131
Make an Ice Cream Stick Puppet	132
About Anwar	
Nasruddin Hodja	133
The Cat and the Tiger	135
Grandma Goes Visiting	137
The Race to the Moon	140
Kalia the Crow	143
Echo and Narcissus	147
Meet the Starfish	151
Foolish Bhola	155
Anwar	158

The Bird's Song

Illustrations :
V.B. Halbe

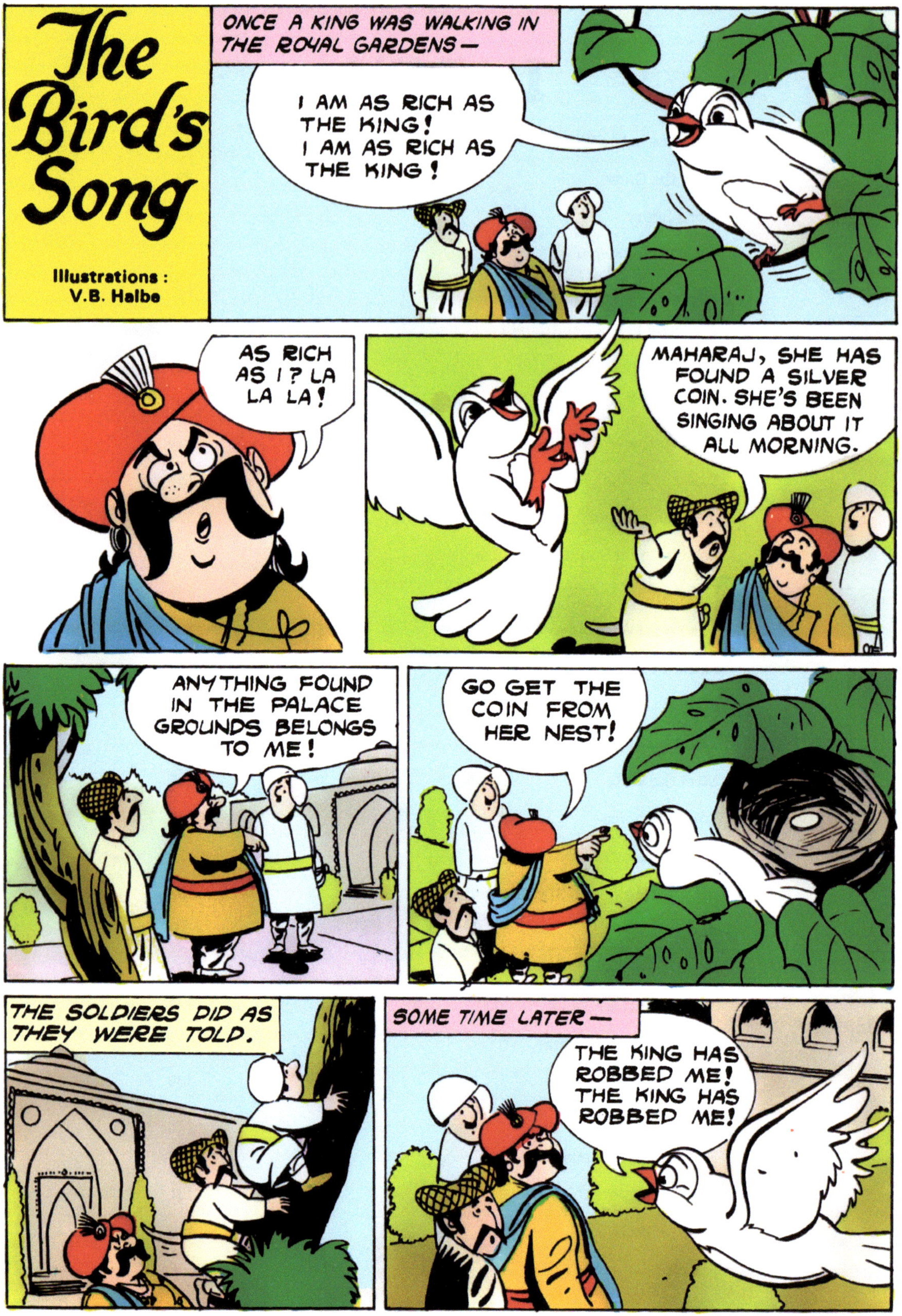

HEY, YOU! THAT WAS MY COIN!
THE KING HAS ROBBED ME...
WHAT A NASTY BIRD! RETURN THAT COIN TO HER OR SHE'LL GIVE ME A BAD NAME!
AGAIN THE SOLDIERS DID AS THEY WERE TOLD.
SOON THE BIRD BEGAN TO SING ANOTHER SONG —
THE KING IS AFRAID OF ME! THE KING IS AFRAID OF ME!
WHAT! SHE THINKS I RETURNED THE COIN BECAUSE I WAS AFRAID OF HER?
CATCH THAT IMPUDENT BIRD!
THE SOLDIERS CAUGHT THE BIRD AND BROUGHT HER TO THE KING.
SO, I'M AFRAID OF YOU, AM I!
GIVE HER TO MY QUEENS. TELL THEM TO FRY HER IN GHEE.
THE KING HAD SEVEN QUEENS. AND THEY WERE DELIGHTED BY THE BIRD.
SHE'S SO CUTE!
LET ME HOLD HER, PLEASE!

NOW GIVE HER TO ME!
AS THE BIRD WAS BEING PASSED FROM HAND TO HAND...
...SHE SUDDENLY PULLED FREE...
...AND FLEW AWAY.
OH!
CATCH HER! CATCH HER!
SHE'S GONE!

A FROG!
WHY DON'T WE COOK IT INSTEAD?
THAT'S A GOOD IDEA!
SO THE QUEENS CAUGHT THE FROG, FRIED IT AND SERVED IT TO THE KING.
IT LOOKS DELICIOUS!
GLOP!
THE FOOLISH CREATURE THOUGHT I WAS AFRAID OF HER... HA, HA, HA!
WHAT FUN! WHAT FUN!
THE KING HAD A FROG FOR LUNCH.
WHAT!

Panel 1: AHHH! SOME WATER! GET ME WATER!

Panel 2: THE KING RINSED HIS MOUTH SEVERAL TIMES.

Panel 3: OH, YOU WRETCHES! YOU FED ME A FROG!

WE... WE...

Panel 4: OFF WITH THEIR NOSES!

SO THE SEVEN QUEENS LOST THEIR NOSES.

Panel 5: AND THE BIRD HAD ANOTHER SONG TO SING—

THE KING'S WIVES HAVE LOST THEIR NOSES...

Panel 6: THE KING'S WIVES HAVE LOST THEIR NOSES... ALL BECAUSE OF A LITTLE BIRD.

Panel 7: THAT BIRD IS DRIVING ME MAD! CATCH HER AGAIN!

"THIS TIME I'LL SWALLOW HER ALIVE."

THE SOLDIERS CAUGHT THE BIRD AND GAVE HER TO THE KING.

GLOOP!

"NO ONE CAN TRIFLE WITH OUR GREAT KING... NOT EVEN A TINY BIRD!"

"I CAN FEEL HER FLUTTERING INSIDE. I MUSTN'T OPEN MY MOUTH..."

"...OR SHE'LL FLY AWAY."

BUT HE COULDN'T HOLD BACK A BELCH.

AND WHEN HE DID —

"CATCH HER! CATCH HER!"

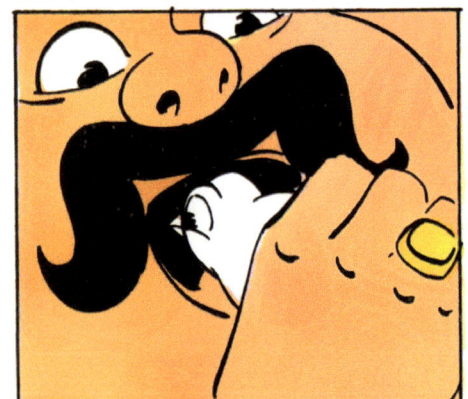

GOT YOU!

GOOD WORK! GIVE HER TO ME!

NOW STAND BY WITH YOUR SWORDS READY.

GLOOP!

GLUB... GLUB... GLUB...

THIS TIME SHE WON'T ESCAPE.

BUT THE BIRD STRUGGLED SO MUCH IN HIS STOMACH.

...THAT HE FELT AN URGE TO BELCH AGAIN.
AND WHEN HE DID —
GRAA-AAH!
SWISH
WHOOOOSH!
CUT HER IN TWO! CUT HER IN TWO!
AAAAAAAAAH!
CALL THE PHYSICIAN.
OH! HOW SAD!
THE KING HAS LOST HIS NOSE! THE KING HAS LOST HIS NOSE!
AND THE BIRD FLEW AWAY AND WAS NEVER SEEN AGAIN.

Nambi and his protruding stomach

Readers' Choice

Based on a story sent by Sanjay Venugopal, Tellicherry
Illustrations: M. Mohandas

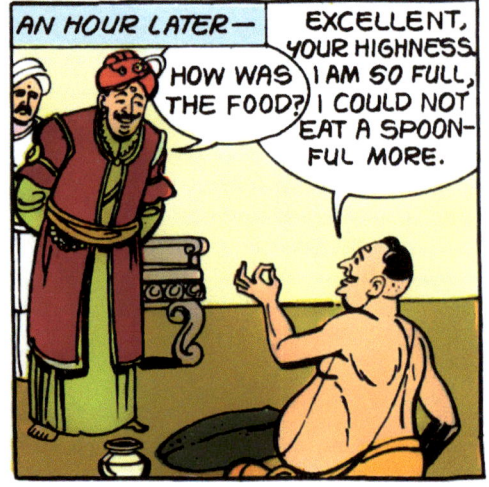

NAMBI WAS KNOWN TO EAT A LOT. ONE DAY HE WAS CALLED TO A FEAST AT THE PALACE...

...AND THERE HE ATE SO MUCH...

...THAT THE KING AND HIS COURTIERS WERE ASTONISHED.

I'VE NEVER SEEN A MAN WITH A GREATER APPETITE.

BRING MORE RICE AND SWEETS. SERVE HIM WELL. HE IS MY SPECIAL GUEST.

MAHARAJ, YOU ARE A KIND HOST.

AN HOUR LATER—

HOW WAS THE FOOD?

EXCELLENT, YOUR HIGHNESS. I AM SO FULL, I COULD NOT EAT A SPOONFUL MORE.

12

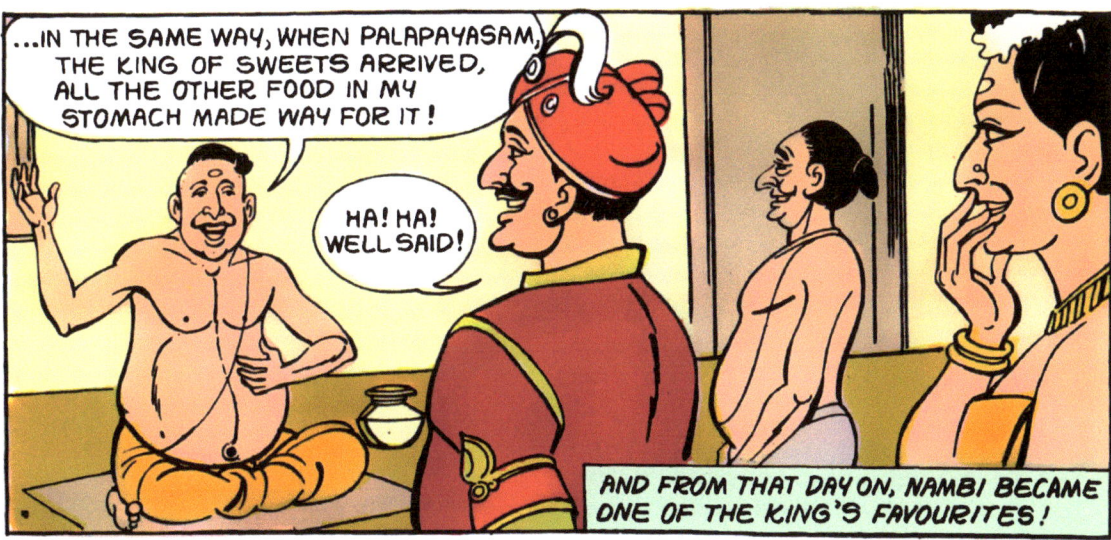

TINKLE TRICKS & TREATS* TTT-33

A What's missing?

B Ramu and Rima saw these fruits growing in an orchard. They were very puzzled. Can you guess why?

C What's wrong with this picture?

* Refer to the footnote under the Editor's Note

SOLUTIONS OF TTT—33

A. There is no gong in the bell.

B. Watermelons are growing on a tree instead of on a creeper. Bananas are growing on a bush instead of on a banana tree. Grapes are growing on a banana tree instead of on a vine. Oranges are growing on a creeper instead of on a tree.

C. The flame should be blue inside and yellow outside.

D Make your own
JAPANESE GARDEN

You will need :
1. A wide bowl
2. A piece of glass
3. Light blue paper
4. Mud
5. Tiny plants - like ferns and those that look like mini-trees.
6. Some pebbles and stones.
7. Some tiny plastic figures and animals and birds. Also a small bridge or house if you have them.

All you have to do is :

Keep the piece of glass in the bowl with the sheet of light blue paper under it. Spread mud all over the glass except in the centre where you want to show the pond. Plant the ferns and the mini-trees in the mud. Place the pebbles and the stones at various places.

Arrange the people, birds, animals and the house and the boat in the garden. You could also make a small bridge and place it across the pond.

Now your Japanese Garden is ready. Show it to your friends and they will all want to make one as well!

EDITOR'S CHOICE

My young friends,

Earth and Clouds

Earth is down,
Clouds are up.
If clouds were down
And earth was up,
How funny the world would look.

My Little Teddy Bear

I have a little teddy bear,
White as snow.
He loves me,
But I don't really know.

These two excellent poems were contributed by Subahi Abbas of Bombay.

Affectionately yours,

Uncle Pai

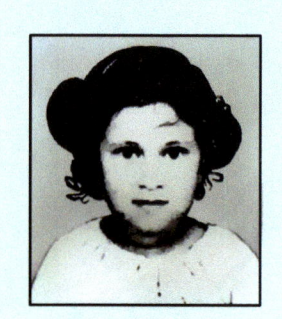

Mooshik
From an idea suggested by Sanjay M. Belurkar, Panaji

To Our Readers*

TINKLE SUBSCRIPTIONS:
All new subscriptions and renewals of the old ones are accepted at:
PARTHA BOOKS DIVISION
Nav Prabhat Chambers, Ranade Road, Dadar, Bombay 400 028.
The annual subscription rate for 24 issues is Rs. 72/- per year (add Rs. 3/- on outstation cheques). Drafts/cheques/M.O. should be in favour of PARTHA BOOKS DIVISION.
All complaints pertaining to the old subscriptions (upto subscription No. 5000) should be addressed to India Book House Magazine Co, 249, D.N. Road, Bombay-400 001.

Readers' Contributions should be addressed to Editor, TINKLE, Mahalaxmi Chambers, (Basement), 22, Bhulabhai Desai Road, Bombay 400 026.

* Send a self-addressed stamped envelope if you want the story to be returned.
* Please do not send photographs until asked for.
* For "Readers' Choice" please send only folk-tales you have heard and not those you have read in books, magazines or textbooks. Rs. 25/- will be paid for every accepted contribution.

Mooshik:
Rs.10/- will be paid for every original idea accepted.

This happened to me:
You can write on your own strange, thrilling, or amusing experience or adventure. Rs. 15/- will be paid for every accepted contribution.

Reader's Mail:
1. Mail your letters to P. Bag No. 16541, Bombay 400 026.
2. Please give your address in your letters, if you want a reply.

TINKLE TRICKS AND TREATS

1. Mail your entry to:
   Tinkle Competition Section,
   P. Bag No. 16541,
   Bombay 400 026.

2. The first 400 all-correct entries received by us will each win a copy of the **Amar India Wall Paper** No. 17 dated September 1983.

* Refer to the footnote under the Editor's Note

CUT HERE

TTT-33

ENTRY FORM*
NAME _____
ADDRESS _____
STATE _____
PIN ☐☐☐☐☐☐

MY SOLUTIONS:
A _____
B _____
C _____

See and Smile
From an idea suggested by Sachi Nath Basak, Patna

Readers Write...

I like reading TINKLE because it always exposes superstitions and wrong beliefs. Please publish more about animals and less about people.

Adil Singh
Hyderabad

In TINKLE No. 29 the piece on the Baya Weaver bird was interesting. But the story sent by Shiv Narayan Malviya, "The Partition", was published earlier in CHANDAMAMA. I request you not to accept stories which have already been published in other children's magazines.

Melvyn N.
Thane

Yours is the best comic I have ever read, but do not increase the price. My pocket money is only Rs. 6/- per month!

Shiv
New Delhi

I am a regular reader of TINKLE and like it for its contribution to science. I wish TINKLE would become a daily.

Prakash Savkoor
Madras

Mooshik
From an idea suggested by Ben Herold, Vizag

MEET THE PRAYING MANTIS

Script: Ashvin
Illustrations: Pradeep Sathe

THIS BEAUTIFUL BUTTERFLY FLUTTERING TOWARDS A FLOWER TO DRINK NECTAR...

...IS CAUGHT BY A STRANGE CREATURE!

THE POOR BUTTERFLY! IT HAD NOT NOTICED THE CREATURE. HAD YOU?

THE CREATURE HOLDS THE BUTTERFLY FIRMLY IN ITS SPINED FORELEGS, DRAWS IT TOWARDS ITS MOUTH...

...AND EATS THE HEAD.

THEN IT REMOVES THE BUTTERFLY'S WINGS AND STARTS CHEWING THE REST OF THE BODY.

AH! FINISHED! BUT THE BUTTERFLY WAS TOO SMALL FOR ITS GREAT APPETITE. SO THE CREATURE SITS ROCK-STILL AND TURNING ITS HEAD SLOWLY, LOOKS FOR OTHER PREY.

NOW YOU'LL UNDERSTAND WHY THE CREATURE IS CALLED A "PRAYING MANTIS" WHEN IT IS ACTUALLY "PREYING". DOESN'T IT LOOK AS IF IT'S PRAYING WITH FOLDED HANDS?

WAIT, WAIT! A SMALL LIZARD IS COMING ITS WAY. THE UNFORTUNATE REPTILE HAS NOT SEEN THE PRAYING MANTIS.
THE INSECT SNAPS IT UP!
... AND BEGINS EATING.
OH, HERE'S AN INSECT-EATING BIRD! THE PRAYING MANTIS TAKES OFF IN A HURRY.
BEING AN INSECT, IT HAS TWO PAIRS OF WINGS, THREE PAIRS OF LEGS, A PAIR OF COMPOUND EYES AND A PAIR OF ANTENNAE, OR FEELERS.
OUR FRIEND ALIGHTS ON A TWIG. LOOK! ANOTHER SMALL MANTIS IS SLOWLY COMING TOWARDS IT.
IT'S A MALE. THE MALES OF THE SPECIES ARE ALWAYS SMALLER THAN THE FEMALES.
THE FEMALE HAS NOTICED HIM, BUT SHE DOESN'T MOVE.
FINALLY, THE MALE COMES VERY, VERY CLOSE ...
... AND THEY MATE.

SOME DAYS LATER THE PREGNANT FEMALE LOOKS FOR A SAFE PLACE TO LAY EGGS.

NOTICE HER SWOLLEN ABDOMEN.

FINALLY, SHE LAYS 80 TO 100 EGGS ON A TWIG. WHILE LAYING THE EGGS SHE SECRETES A LIQUID.

THE LIQUID HARDENS AND DRIES ENCLOSING THE EGGS WITHIN IT.

EGG-CASES

AFTER LAYING THE EGGS THE FEMALE WALKS AWAY. SHE DOESN'T HAVE TO WORRY BECAUSE HER EGGS ARE SAFE IN THE CAPSULE. THE TOUGH, SPONGY CAPSULE CHANGES COLOUR TO SUIT ITS BACKGROUND.

AFTER SOME DAYS, THE EGGS HATCH AND THE BABY MANTISES COME OUT.

THEY LOOK LIKE ADULTS BUT ARE SMALLER IN SIZE AND THEY DON'T HAVE WINGS.

THEY ARE AS GLUTTONOUS AS THE ADULTS AND MOST OF THEIR TIME IS SPENT IN TRYING TO CATCH OTHER INSECTS.

THEY GROW BY GRADUAL STAGES, MOULTING UPTO 12 TIMES BEFORE BECOMING ADULTS.

THE PRAYING MANTIS, WHICH YOU HAVE JUST MET IS FOUND IN OUR COUNTRY.

HERE IS ITS AFRICAN COUSIN.

IT HAS BIG 'EYES' ON ITS WINGS TO FRIGHTEN AWAY ENEMIES.

THIS IS AN ORCHID MANTIS FOUND IN MALAYSIA. ITS BODY, EVEN ITS LEGS LOOK LIKE THE PETALS OF AN ORCHID.

THE RELATIVE OF THE PRAYING MANTIS IS THE COCKROACH. COCKROACHES TOO LAY THEIR EGGS IN CAPSULES LIKE THE MANTIS. YOU HAVE PROBABLY SEEN THEIR CAPSULES OR EGG-CASES.

The Fee

story: P. Varadarajan
Illustrations: Prabhakar Patil

ONE DAY, RAMU WAS GOING TO THE FAIR IN HIS DONKEY-CART, TO BUY RICE...

WHEN —

OH! THERE'S THE TOLL-KEEPER OF THE BRIDGE.

NOW I'LL HAVE TO PAY THE TOLL FEE OF ONE RUPEE TO CROSS OVER.

HMM...

SUDDENLY, RAMU GOT DOWN FROM HIS CART AND UNHARNESSED HIS DONKEY.

THEN RAMU SET OFF AGAIN.
AT THE BRIDGE —
YOU, THERE! WHERE'S YOUR TOLL FEE?
ASK THE DRIVER.
THEN —
HA, HA, HA, HA!
SO AMUSED WAS THE TOLL-KEEPER THAT HE MOVED ASIDE...
... AND LET RAMU CROSS OVER WITHOUT CHARGING HIM THE FEE.

THE MOON — Our Strange Neighbour — 2

Script: J.D. Isloor • Illustrations: Anand Mande

WE ARE USED TO BLUE SKIES...

BUT DID YOU KNOW THAT THE SKY OVER THE MOON IS PITCH BLACK EVEN DURING THE DAY? IT'S BECAUSE THERE'S NO AIR THERE.

OUR EARTH HAS A BLANKET OF AIR AROUND IT. THIS BLANKET OF AIR IS CALLED THE ATMOSPHERE.
THE ATMOSPHERE MAKES OUR SKY LOOK BLUE.
AND IT DOES MANY OTHER THINGS BESIDES.
IN THE DAYTIME IT SHIELDS THE EARTH FROM THE SUN'S HEAT AND AT NIGHT IT PREVENTS HEAT FROM THE EARTH FROM ESCAPING INTO SPACE.

THE POOR MOON HAS NO ATMOSPHERE TO PROTECT IT.
DURING THE DAY THE SUN BEATS DOWN MERCILESSLY AND DIRECTLY ON THE MOON'S SURFACE AND THE TEMPERATURE GOES OVER THE BOILING POINT. IF A MAN WERE SUDDENLY TO FIND HIMSELF ON THE MOON, HIS BLOOD WOULD BOIL IN THE HEAT...

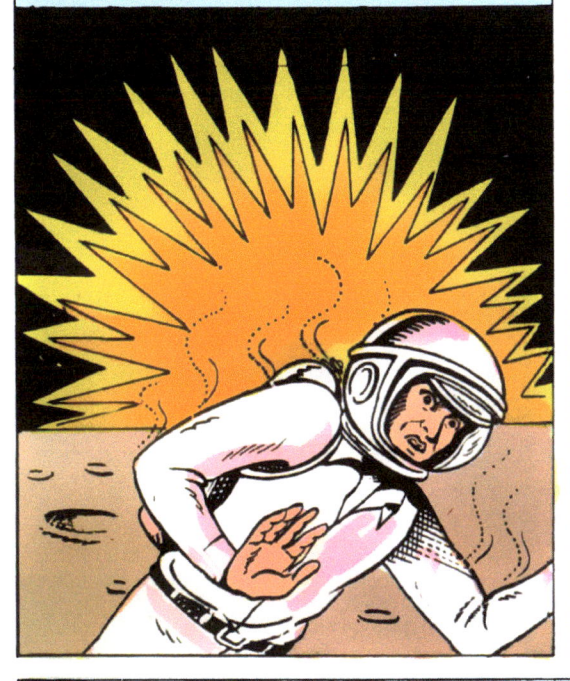

...HE WOULD LEAP INTO A SHADED PLACE...

...AND THERE HE WOULD SHIVER WITH COLD.

ON EARTH, HEAT IS CARRIED FROM ONE PLACE TO ANOTHER BY AIR. AS THERE IS NO AIR ON THE MOON, HEAT STAYS WHERE IT IS WITHOUT SPREADING AROUND.
THE AREA EXPOSED TO SUNLIGHT BECOMES VERY, VERY HOT.
BUT SHADED PLACES REMAIN BITTERLY COLD.
THE WHOLE LAND BECOMES BITTERLY COLD, THE MOMENT THE SUN GOES DOWN.
AT MIDNIGHT THE TEMPERATURE ON THE MOON IS $-150°C$.

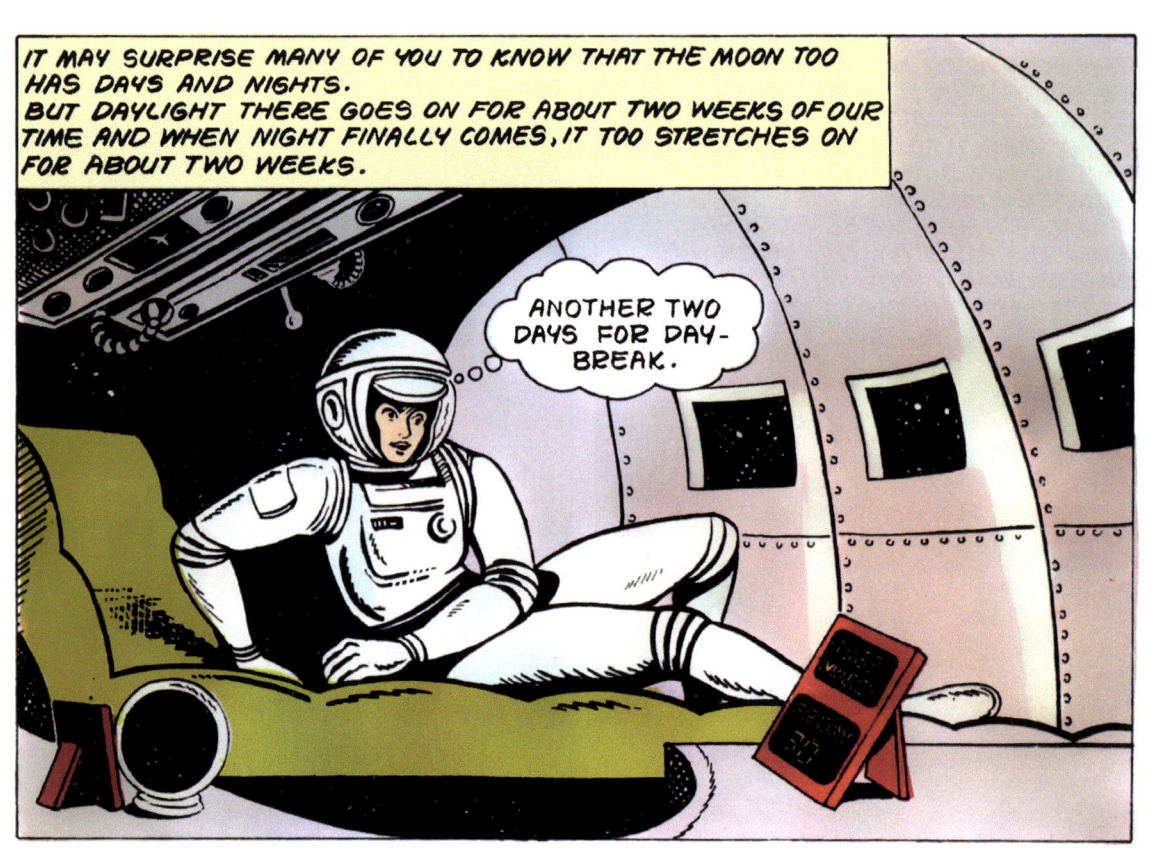

IT MAY SURPRISE MANY OF YOU TO KNOW THAT THE MOON TOO HAS DAYS AND NIGHTS.
BUT DAYLIGHT THERE GOES ON FOR ABOUT TWO WEEKS OF OUR TIME AND WHEN NIGHT FINALLY COMES, IT TOO STRETCHES ON FOR ABOUT TWO WEEKS.

ANOTHER TWO DAYS FOR DAYBREAK.

WE GET MOONLIGHT AT NIGHT. WHAT DOES THE MOON GET? EARTHLIGHT.
EARTH, LIKE THE MOON, DOES NOT HAVE ANY LIGHT OF ITS OWN, BUT IT REFLECTS SUNLIGHT. AND IT REFLECTS IT BETTER THAN THE MOON DOES.
YOU COULD READ A PAPER VERY COMFORTABLY IN EARTHLIGHT.

Kalia
THE CROW
Script:
LUIS
Illustrations :
PRADEEP SATHE
THIS GRASS IS SO JUICY AND SWEET.
WHAT'S THAT? I THOUGHT I HEARD A SOUND.
BANG
HUNTERS!
OOOPS!
I THINK I GOT HIM.
YES, HE'S LIMPING.
DON'T SHOOT! A LIVE DEER SHOULD FETCH US A BETTER PRICE THAN A DEAD ONE. I'LL RUN AFTER HIM AND CATCH HIM.

HE'S CHASING ME.
RUN, SHONAR, RUN!
GO! GO!
FASTER!
HE'S GAINING ON ME.
OH-OH, SHONAR IS IN TROUBLE.
HEY!
COME BACK WITH MY HAT, YOU DIRTY CROW!

YOU...!

AAAH!

HE'S COMING AFTER ME NOW...!

A C-CROCODILE!

ARE YOU ALL RIGHT?

BRRR... BRRR...

MY HAT!

COME BACK WITH MY HAT YOU MISERABLE JACKAL!

NOT A CHANCE! THIS HAT IS JUST WHAT I WANTED!

NO.40
Rs. 3
TINKLE
AMAR CHITRA KATHA
THE FORTNIGHTLY FOR CHILDREN FROM THE HOUSE OF AMAR CHITRA KATHA
MEET THE PRAYING MANTIS
(Can you find the Mantis in this picture?)
THE BIRD'S SONG

SAY HELLO TO

DILIP KADAM

Thousands of pages of *Amar Chitra Katha* (ACK) and *Tinkle* owe their existence to the expert hands of Mr. Dilip Kadam. His art has the power to transport you to another time and place.

Mr. Kadam has worked on numerous books—right from brilliant ACK books such as *Tales of Shivaji* and *Lokmanya Tilak*, to memorable *Tinkle* stories such as 'The Olive Jar' and 'The Hunchback of Kashgar'.

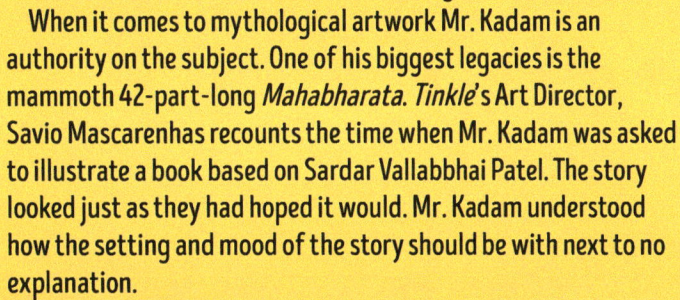

When it comes to mythological artwork Mr. Kadam is an authority on the subject. One of his biggest legacies is the mammoth 42-part-long *Mahabharata*. *Tinkle*'s Art Director, Savio Mascarenhas recounts the time when Mr. Kadam was asked to illustrate a book based on Sardar Vallabbhai Patel. The story looked just as they had hoped it would. Mr. Kadam understood how the setting and mood of the story should be with next to no explanation.

He says, in all his years as an artist, there's never been a time when he was at a loss to come up with a fresh new character. His grasp of human anatomy and behavior is stunning. A major reason for this is because he believes that his characters have a life of their own, independent of the books they appear in.

Mr. Kadam's favourite character to draw has been Bhim from *Mahabharata*. According to him, Bhim, while being extraordinary, was one of the most relatable characters in the epic.

Along with being a comic artist, Mr. Kadam is also a painter. His paintings are admired all through the country. He has received the President's Award—given to him by the then President of India, Gyani Zail Singh—for his contribution to the world of art.

Today Mr. Kadam runs his own comic studio in Pune. He has also created sketch books to guide young and aspiring artists. He urges new parents to take their kids to art exhibitions as they would take them for a movie. He believes then will our country grow to appreciate art in its true form.

Adventures Of KASPERLE

A folktale from Germany
Script: **Sarla Mehta**
Illustrations: **V.B. Halbe**

Walking through the forest, Kasperle stopped to read a sign.

WANTED NIGHT WATCHMAN FOR THE KING

Why are you here, Your Majesty?

Yesterday a wicked witch cast a spell over my daughter at this very spot.

My daughter disappeared. But I know she is here somewhere.

That's why I need someone to keep a watch here.

I will gladly stand guard for you, Your Majesty.

Then please start your duties now. I will return with my soldiers to make a search of the forest.

29

30

THE CROCODILE APPEARED WHEN I WAS NEAR THIS FLOWER.
I MUST TAKE A CLOSER LOOK AT IT.
DON'T TOUCH THAT FLOWER, OR I'LL KILL YOU!
THERE'S CERTAINLY SOMETHING FISHY ABOUT THAT FLOWER.
I DIDN'T MEAN ANY HARM, SIR.
BUT THE FLOWER HAS SUCH A LOVELY PERFUME. TAKE A SNIFF.
GOOD THING I HAD THAT SNEEZING POWDER WITH ME!

AAH...AH...

...TISHOO...

AH... TISHOO!

THERE'S SOMETHING ABOUT THIS FLOWER...

LEAVE THAT FLOWER ALONE!

MR. DEVIL, I'M GUARDING THIS FLOWER FOR MY FRIEND THE GHOST. HE CAUGHT A COLD AND IS SNEEZING THERE.

AAA... TISHOO!

OH THAT'S ALL RIGHT THEN! GUARD THE FLOWER WELL TILL THE WITCH COMES.

WITCH? NOW I'M SURE THE PRINCESS HAS BEEN TURNED INTO THAT FLOWER.

OH, OH, HERE COMES THE WITCH! I'D BETTER HIDE.

HEE HEE HEE! HOW ARE YOU MY LITTLE PRINCESS?

I MUST SEE YOUR LOVELY FACE AGAIN.

ABRACADABRA, POWER AND MIGHT, FLOWER TURN INTO PRINCESS BRIGHT!

HEE HEE HEE! MY LOVELY PRISONER! YOU WILL BE MY DINNER TONIGHT.
WILL NOBODY HELP ME?
I WILL HELP YOU, PRINCESS.
ABRACADABRA, MIGHT AND POWER, WITCH TURN INTO UGLY FLOWER!
NO!
!
OH THANK YOU, THANK YOU!
DAUGHTER!
THANK GOD YOU'RE SAFE!
THE KING REWARDED KASPERLE HANDSOMELY FOR RESCUING HIS DAUGHTER.

SPEED

Script: Luis M. Fernandes
Illustrations: Anand Mande

Our fastest runners can run 1.5 kilometres in less than four minutes.

But a horse can run the same distance in only a little more than a minute and a half.

The horse, however, is slow compared to a cheetah.

A cheetah can cover a kilometre in less than 40 seconds.

But a hawk can fly more than twice as fast as a cheetah can run.

THE FASTEST LIVING THINGS, HOWEVER, ARE NO MATCH FOR THE MACHINES MAN HAS BUILT.

TODAY, ROCKETS ARE MAN'S FASTEST MACHINES... SOME OF THEM CAN TRAVEL AT SEVERAL TIMES THE SPEED OF SOUND (SOUND TRAVELS AT ABOUT 1200 KM. PER HOUR).

THE ROCKETS THAT TAKE SPACECRAFTS OUT OF THE EARTH'S GRAVITY, TRAVEL AT AROUND 40,000 KM PER HOUR.

BUT EVEN THE FASTEST ROCKETS ARE SLOW COMPARED TO THE SPEED AT WHICH THE EARTH WHIRLS ROUND THE SUN. IT TRAVELS AT NEARLY 1,800 KM PER MINUTE.

HOWEVER, EVEN THIS SPEED IS NOTHING COMPARED TO THE SPEED OF LIGHT. LIGHT TRAVELS AT 299,792 KM IN ONE SECOND!

MAN HAS YET TO BUILD A MACHINE THAT CAN TRAVEL AT THAT SPEED.

Shikari Shambu

Script:
Luis M. Fernandes

Illustrations:
V.B. Halbe

* Refer to the footnote under the Editor's Note

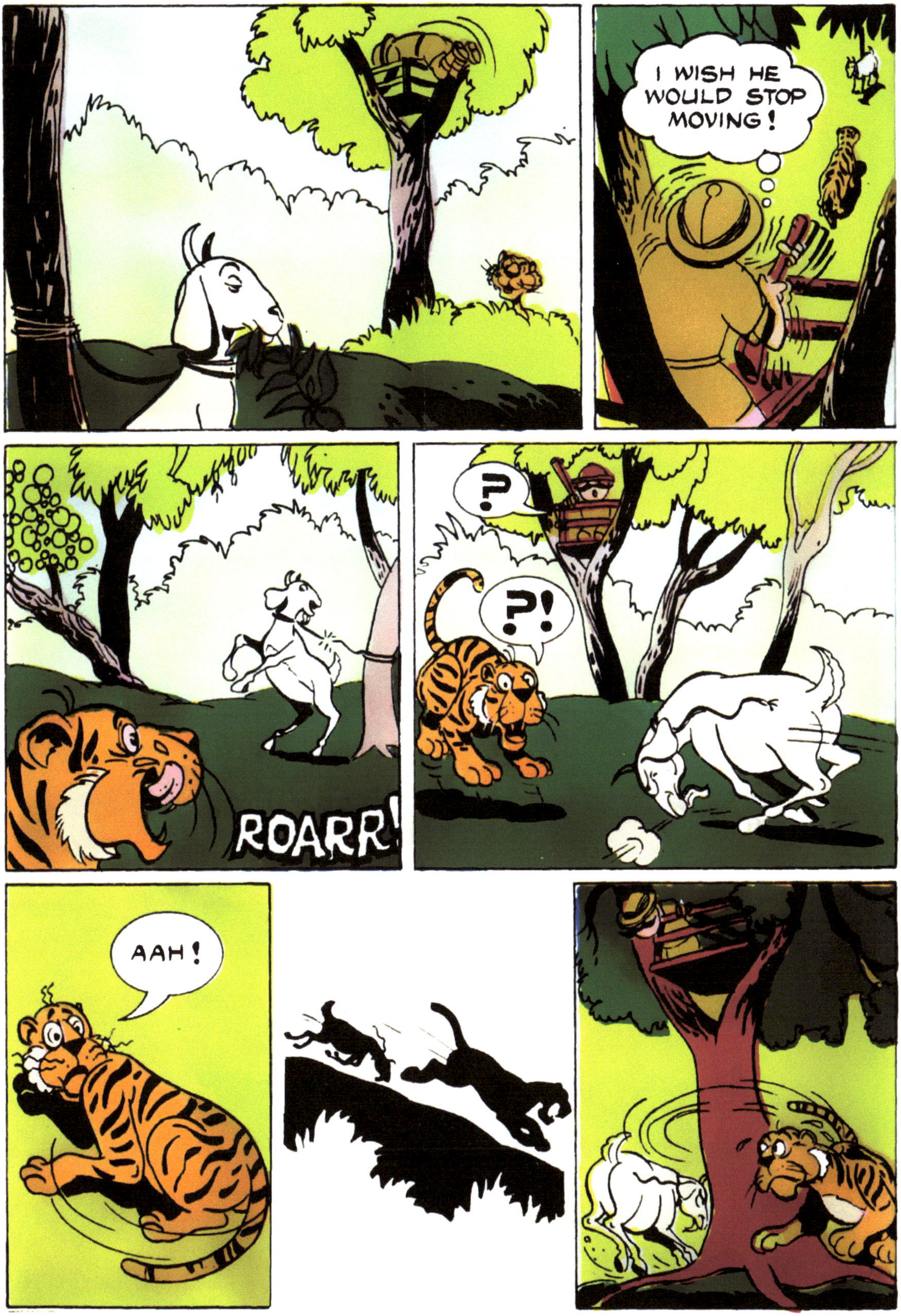
I WISH HE WOULD STOP MOVING!
ROARR!
?
?!
AAH!

39

THE DONKEY AND THE LION

Story: J.S. Iyer
Illustrations: M. Mohandas

ONE DAY, A DONKEY WAS GRAZING IN A FOREST.

THE GRASS IS SO SWEET AND PLENTIFUL HERE.

SUDDENLY—

WHAT ARE YOU DOING HERE?

YIEEEE! P-PLEASE D-DON'T EAT ME, SIR!

I'VE HAD SUCH A HEAVY MEAL. I'M FEELING VERY DROWSY...

HOW STRANGE! HE'S NOT ATTACKING ME!

I THINK HE'S AFRAID OF ME!

IF HE IS AFRAID OF ME, THEN I SHOULD BE MADE KING OF THIS FOREST.

COME HERE, EVERYBODY! COME HERE!

WHEN ALL THE ANIMALS HAD ASSEMBLED—

"FROM TODAY I AM THE KING OF THIS JUNGLE!"

"HOW CAN THAT BE?"

"...THE LION IS OUR KING."

"NOT ANY MORE, HE'S AFRAID OF ME."

"THAT'S UNBELIEVABLE."

"ALL RIGHT. I SHALL PROVE IT."

THE ANIMALS WATCHED FROM A SAFE DISTANCE AS THE DONKEY WALKED BOLDLY UP TO THE LION.

"SEE HOW QUIETLY HE LIES AT MY FEET."

"YOU MUST DO BETTER THAN THAT. WHY DON'T YOU KICK HIM TO PROVE YOU ARE STRONGER!"

!

"ROARRRR!"

AT THE LION'S ROAR, THE DONKEY SHOOK WITH FEAR...

...AND RAN FOR HIS LIFE.

"HA! HA! HE WANTED TO BE KING!!"

"HA! HA!"

"LOOK AT HIM GO."

ANWAR
by
Appaswami
Illustrations: V. B. Halbe
I WANT YOU TO KNOW THE IMPORTANCE OF INDEPENDENCE DAY...
THE COUNTRY BECAME INDEPENDENT ON... BLAH ... BLAH... BLAH...
LATER—
NOW ALL OF YOU WILL GET TOFFEES.
WOW!
NOW... ONE AT A TIME... ONE AT A TIME...
AT HOME—
ANWAR, DID YOUR TEACHER TELL YOU ABOUT THE IMPORTANCE OF INDEPENDENCE DAY?
NEWS
YES, BABA.
TODAY WE ARE ALLOWED TO SPOIL OUR TEETH.
?
NEWS
THE TEACHER HERSELF GIVES US TOFFEES ON IND... IND... IND... PEND... DAY!
!

Readers Write...*

In TINKLE No. 33 the story, The Phantom Car, has a car moving because the driver is pushing it from behind. But will a car move in the correct direction unless someone handles the steering wheel?

A.G. Prathab
Bangalore

(It won't! You're very observant. *Editor*)

A few days ago I received my copy of TINKLE. I read just half of it and rushed off to school. When I returned I couldn't find it so I asked my father if he knew where it was. He told me to go and ask my mother since she knows where everything is in the house. But do you know he was reading my copy of TINKLE all that time?

Aloke Chawla
Bombay

I'm glad that TINKLE is now a fortnightly. Why don't you include features on rare metals and plants?

Y. Srinivas
Madras

(We are planning a feature on plants. *Editor*)

Mooshik

From an idea suggested by Abhijeet P. Sharma, Surat

We usually make a lot of sound. But sound is energy and we should try to conserve it. Sound pollutes the air so we must avoid making it.

N.B. Sanjeev
Hyderabad

* Refer to the footnote under the Editor's Note

See and Smile

DID YOU KNOW?

Polo is one of the world's oldest games. It was being played in Persia (Iran) at least 2,500 years ago. From Persia it spread to Arabia and from there to Tibet, China and Japan.

It is recorded that in 910 A.D. a relative of the Chinese emperor, T'ai Tsu, died while playing the game and the emperor had all the other players beheaded.

The game reached India by the 13th century. From India the game was carried to England. And from there it spread all over the world.

The first Europeans to play polo were British tea planters in Assam. They had learnt the game in nearby Manipur.

International rules for playing were drawn up in 1939.

Polo is very much like hockey except that it is played on horseback. And there are only four members in each team. The teams change ends after each goal.

SAY IT YOURSELF AND WIN A CASH PRIZE* NO. 2

ICE-CREAM

I'LL DUCK OUT OF SIGHT... OR I'LL HAVE TO SHARE MY ICE-CREAM WITH MANI.

BUT THERE'S A PUDDLE IN HIS PATH AND...

SPLASH!

WHAT DO YOU THINK MANI IS SAYING?

* Refer to the footnote under the Editor's Note

1. Mail your entry to:
   TINKLE
   Competition Section,
   P. Bag No. 16541
   Bombay 400 026

2. ● First prize — Rs. 50/-
   ● Second prize — Rs. 25/-
   ● Third prize — Rs. 15/-
   ● 10 Consolation prizes, — Rs. 10/- each

3. Decision of the judges is final and binding. Names of the prize-winners will be announced in TINKLE No. 45 dated 20th October, 1983.

Last date for receiving entries: September 20, 1983

------- CUT HERE

ENTRY FORM*   Say it Yourself – 2

NAME _____   Answer: _____

ADDRESS _____

STATE _____

PIN _____

45

MEET THE DOLPHIN

Script : Ashvin
Illustrations : Pradeep Sathe

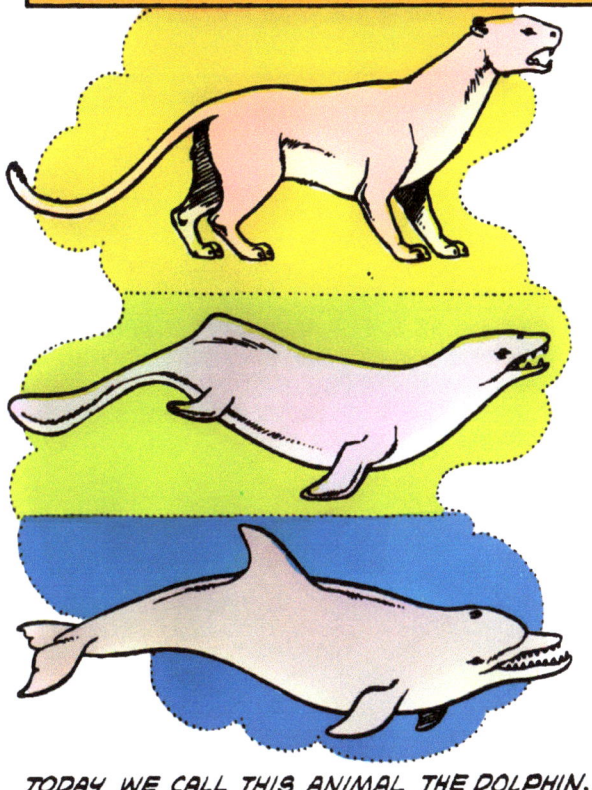

SOME 50 MILLION YEARS AGO THERE WAS AN ANIMAL WHICH LIVED ON LAND, BUT FED ON FISH AND OTHER SEA CREATURES.

THIS LED TO IT SPENDING A LOT OF TIME IN WATER. AND GRADUALLY IT BEGAN TO CHANGE INTO A WATER ANIMAL.

THE CHANGE DID NOT TAKE PLACE SUDDENLY, BUT VERY, VERY SLOWLY AND OVER A PERIOD OF MILLIONS OF YEARS.

TODAY WE CALL THIS ANIMAL THE DOLPHIN.

THE DOLPHIN LOOKS LIKE A FISH, BUT IT IS A MAMMAL.

THAT IS WHY IT CANNOT BREATHE UNDERWATER LIKE A FISH...

...AND HAS SKIN ON ITS BODY AND NOT SCALES.

ITS TAIL-FLUKES ARE HORIZONTAL AND NOT VERTICAL LIKE THE TAIL-FINS OF THE FISH.

FISH MOVE THROUGH WATER BY BENDING THEIR ENTIRE BODIES IN S-SHAPED CURVES.

THE DOLPHIN SWIMS WITH THE HELP OF UP AND DOWN STROKES MADE BY ITS TAIL-FLUKES.

HERE IS A SCHOOL (GROUP) OF BOTTLENOSE DOLPHINS LOOKING FOR FOOD. THEY FEED ON FISH.

THEY HAVE 80 TO 90 CONICAL TEETH TO HELP THEM CATCH THE SLIPPERY PREY.

BUT THEY CAN STAY UNDERWATER FOR ONLY A FEW MINUTES. THEN THEY MUST SURFACE TO BREATHE. THEIR NOSTRILS ARE ON THEIR FOREHEADS.

IT'S RESTING TIME. THESE FEMALES ARE HAVING A QUIET SNOOZE. THEY'RE SLEEPING WITH THEIR NOSTRILS EXPOSED TO AIR SO THAT THEY CAN BREATHE.

THE MALES SLEEP ABOUT A FOOT BELOW THE SURFACE. EVERY FIVE MINUTES THEY COME UP, OPEN THEIR NOSTRILS, BREATHE, CLOSE THEIR NOSTRILS AND GO DOWN AGAIN. THIS IS A REFLEX ACTION AND DOES NOT DISTURB THEIR SLEEP.

THE ADULT MALE IS ABOUT 4 M. LONG.

THE FEMALE IS ABOUT 3 1/4 M. LONG. THEY MATE IN WATER.

A YEAR LATER THE FEMALE GIVES BIRTH TO ONE BABY. IT IS BORN TAIL FIRST...

...AND AS SOON AS IT'S BORN, THE MOTHER HELPS IT TO SURFACE TO TAKE ITS FIRST BREATH.

THEN THE BABY GOES DOWN TO THE UNDERSIDE OF ITS MOTHER'S BODY FOR ITS FIRST FEED — MILK. SINCE DOLPHINS ARE MAMMALS, THE FEMALES HAVE TEATS. THEY ARE IN A GROOVE NEAR HER TAIL. THE MOTHER SQUIRTS THE MILK IN THE BABY'S MOUTH. AFTER EVERY GULP THE YOUNG ONE HAS TO SURFACE TO BREATHE. IT CANNOT HOLD ITS BREATH AS LONG AS ADULT DOLPHINS.

FOR A YEAR THE BABY FEEDS ONLY ON MOTHER'S MILK. LATER, IT TRIES SOLID FOOD.

THE ADULTS PROTECT THE YOUNG. IF DANGER THREATENS, SAY IN THE FORM OF A SHARK, ALL THE ADULTS GET TOGETHER TO DRIVE THE SHARK AWAY FROM THE YOUNG ONES.

IF THE MOTHER DOLPHIN DIES, ANOTHER FEMALE OF THE GROUP WILL ADOPT THE ORPHAN BABY.

DOLPHINS ARE GENERALLY PLAYFUL AND PEACE-LOVING. THEY PLAY AND TEASE EACH OTHER A LOT AND SOME BOLD DOLPHINS EVEN PLAY WITH HUMAN SWIMMERS.

THEIR FAVOURITE GAME IS TO JUMP HIGH INTO THE AIR. A 4-METRE BOTTLENOSE DOLPHIN CAN LEAP UPTO 7 METRES IN THE AIR!

SOMETIMES THEY SWIM AROUND SHIPS, SHOWING OFF WITH MANY ACROBATIC TRICKS AND ARE REWARDED WITH SCRAPS OF FOOD BY THE SAILORS.

AFTER EATING THIS FOOD, THEY ARE KNOWN TO MAKE MANY DIFFERENT SOUNDS LIKE WHISTLES, SQUAWKS AND QUACKS.

DOLPHINS HAVE POOR EYE-SIGHT AND PROBABLY NO SENSE OF SMELL. THEY FIND THEIR PREY AND CAN SWIM AROUND WITHOUT BUMPING INTO OBSTACLES BECAUSE OF THEIR WONDERFUL SENSE OF HEARING. LIKE BATS THEY MAKE SHRILL SOUNDS. SO SHRILL THAT THEY CANNOT BE HEARD BY HUMAN EARS. THESE SOUNDS BOUNCE BACK FROM OBJECTS IN THEIR PATH. THE SOUNDS WHICH BOUNCE BACK OR ECHOES AS THEY ARE CALLED, ENABLE THE DOLPHINS TO KNOW WHAT IS AHEAD AND AROUND THEM.

A BOAT'S HULL

DOLPHINS HAVE A LANGUAGE OF THEIR OWN. AS WE USE WORDS, THEY USE SOUNDS. THEY HAVE A WIDE VOCABULARY OF SOUNDS.

HUMAN EARS CANNOT HEAR ALL THESE SOUNDS.

BUT SCIENTISTS ARE TRYING TO LEARN THE LANGUAGE OF THE DOLPHINS WITH THE HELP OF SPECIAL EQUIPMENT.

PERHAPS ONE DAY WE SHALL BE ABLE TO TALK TO THESE FRIENDLY, INTELLIGENT ANIMALS IN THEIR OWN LANGUAGE.

HERE ARE TWO SPECIES OF DOLPHINS FOUND IN INDIA:

THE COMMON DOLPHIN (2½ M. LONG)
FOUND IN THE BAY OF BENGAL AND THE INDIAN OCEAN.

THE GANGETIC DOLPHIN (2 M. LONG)
FOUND IN THE RIVERS GANGA AND THE BRAHMAPUTRA.

THE DOLPHIN (FISH)
THE DOLPHIN FISH IS NOT TO BE CONFUSED WITH THE DOLPHINS WE'VE JUST READ ABOUT.

THIS DOLPHIN IS A FISH. ANOTHER NAME FOR IT IS 'DORADO'.

The Day Jalebies Grew On Trees

READERS' CHOICE

Bassd on a story sent by
Sumon Bhattacharjee, Shillong
Illustrations: Ram Waeerkar

AND YET WHEN THE FARMER GOT UP AFTER A SHORT NAP.
KEEP THIS TO YOURSELF, PLEASE...
OF COURSE!
OH, THAT WOMAN!
THE FARMER WENT TO A SWEETMEAT SHOP AND BOUGHT A MOUND OF SWEETS.
MITHAI
THEN HE WENT TO THE NEARBY WOODS AND HUNG THE SWEETS ON THE TREES.
FINALLY, HE RETURNED HOME—
WIFE! COME QUICKLY!
WHERE?
COME WITH ME FOR A SHORT WALK IN THE WOODS.
YOU'LL SEE SUCH STRANGE SIGHTS! COME ON!

IN THE WOODS—

OH... OH!

MM... MMM!

I NEVER KNEW JALEBIS GREW ON TREES.

WHEN THEY RETURNED HOME THAT EVENING...

...THEY FOUND THE RAJA ON THEIR DOORSTEP.

WHERE IS THE POT OF GOLD?

POT OF GOLD! WHICH POT OF GOLD?

HOW DID YOU HEAR ABOUT THIS POT, MAHARAJ?

ASK YOUR WIFE! SHE TOLD EVERYBODY.

OH, MY WIFE IS ALWAYS TELLING TALL TALES, MAHARAJ.

...IN FACT SHE IS...ER ...SLIGHTLY...
WHAT!... I AM MAD... AM I?
WHAT CHEEK! WITH MY OWN EYES I SAW THAT POT OF GOLD...
...JUST AS I SAW THOSE JALEBIS AND LADDOOS GROWING ON TREES TODAY! SAY THAT WAS NONSENSE TOO!
MOST DELICIOUS JALEBIS YOU EVER ATE!
DID YOU HEAR THAT, MY LORD?
AND THE SIZE OF THE LADDOOS WAS...
BE QUIET, YOU STUPID WOMAN!
COME ON, WE HAVE WASTED ENOUGH TIME!

OH AND EH!

A folktale from Kashmir

Script : Navina Venkat
Illustrations : M. Mohandas

I WOULD LIKE TO SEE HOW MY FAMILY IS GETTING ON.
HE DOES THE WORK OF THREE PEOPLE HERE. WHO WILL DO HIS WORK IF I LET HIM GO?
I'LL LET YOU GO IF YOU GET ME TWO THINGS FROM THE MARKET...
CERTAINLY, SAHIB.
WHAT DO YOU WANT ME TO GET?
'OH' AND 'EH'.
'OH' AND 'EH'?
YES, 'OH' AND 'EH'!
HERE'S THE MONEY.

I WONDER WHAT 'EH' AND 'OH' ARE !
PLEASE GIVE ME SOME 'EH' AND 'OH'.
'EH' AND 'OH'?
GET AWAY FROM HERE, YOU FOOL!
AZIZ WAS DRIVEN AWAY FROM EVERY SHOP HE WENT TO.
FINALLY —
I'LL TRY AT THIS LAST SHOP.
SIR, I-I WANT SOME... SOME...
...SOME 'EH' AND 'OH'.
YES?
'EH' AND 'OH'?
YES, THE KHWAJA SAHIB HAS SENT ME TO GET THEM.
THE KHWAJA SAHIB, EH?
I KNOW HIM WELL.
TOO WELL! THE ROGUE IS DEFINITELY TRYING TO CHEAT THIS POOR MAN IN SOME WAY.

AS A MATTER OF FACT, I DO HAVE WHAT YOU WANT. WAIT HERE.
THE OLD MAN WENT INTO THE NEXT ROOM AND SOON RETURNED WITH TWO POTS.
HERE YOU ARE.
ONE POT OF 'EH'...
...AND ONE OF 'OH'. LET THE KHWAJA SAHIB OPEN THE POTS HIMSELF.
HERE'S THE MONEY.
AZIZ BUTH RUSHED BACK WITH THE POTS.
MASTER, I'VE GOT THEM!
WHAT ?

Panel 1:
"THE 'EH' AND 'OH'."
"REALLY?"

Panel 2:
"YES. NOW PLEASE LET ME GO."
"LET ME SEE IF YOU'VE BROUGHT THE RIGHT THINGS FIRST."

Panel 3:
"I WONDER WHAT HE HAS BROUGHT."

Panel 4:
"EH!"
"A MOSQUITO!"

Panel 5:
"IS THAT 'EH'? THEN THE OTHER MUST BE 'OH'."

OH!
A BEE!
NOW THAT I'VE BROUGHT YOU 'EH' AND 'OH', CAN I GO AWAY, SAHIB?
MY GUESTS ARE BEGINNING TO WONDER WHAT'S GOING ON. I'D BETTER LET THIS FOOL GO.
ALL RIGHT... GO!
THANK YOU! SAHIB! THANK YOU!
BUT COME BACK SOON, YOU HEAR!
BUT AZIZ WAS ALREADY OUT OF EARSHOT.

MEET THE GOLDEN EAGLE

Script: Ashvin
Illustrations: Pradeep Sathe

THE GOLDEN EAGLE IS FOUND IN SEVERAL PLACES NORTH OF THE EQUATOR WHERE THERE ARE MOUNTAINS.

IN INDIA THEY ARE FOUND IN THE HIMALAYAS AT A HEIGHT OF 1220 METRES.

THEY LIVE IN PAIRS. HERE IS A PAIR SOARING MAJESTICALLY IN THE AIR. THEY DON'T FLAP THEIR WINGS TOO MUCH, BUT JUST GLIDE IN THE AIR. IN THIS WAY THEY AVOID TIRING THEMSELVES AND THEY CAN STAY UP FOR HOURS TOGETHER.

EACH PAIR LIVES AND HUNTS IN A TERRITORY OF ABOUT 32 SQ. Km. OTHER EAGLES ARE NOT ALLOWED TO ENTER THIS TERRITORY.

BUT BIRDS WHICH THEY CAN CATCH FOR FOOD ARE ALWAYS WELCOME. THIS MAGPIE HAS WANDERED INTO THEIR TERRITORY.

ONE OF THE EAGLES DIVES AT TERRIFIC SPEED WITH HALF-FOLDED WINGS...

...REACHES OUT WITH ITS TALONS...

...AND GRABS THE BIRD.

THE DEAD BIRD IS TAKEN TO A FAVOURITE EATING PLACE.

WELL DONE, HIS MATE SEEMS TO SAY.

SHE IS LARGER AND HEAVIER THAN HIM.

THEY PLUCK THEIR PREY WITH THEIR HOOKED BEAKS, RIP THE FLESH INTO PIECES AND SWALLOW THEM WHOLE.

BUT THE MAGPIE WAS TOO SMALL. HERE THEY GO AGAIN LOOKING FOR MORE FOOD.

A MAN LOOKING DOWN FROM A HELICOPTER WOULD NOT SEE ANYTHING ON THE GROUND HERE. BUT THE EAGLES HAVE SEEN A RABBIT. THEY CAN SEE WELL EVEN FROM A DISTANCE OF 250 METRES.

AS THE PREY IS BIG AND HEAVY, IT IS THE LARGER BIRD, THE FEMALE, WHO DIVES THIS TIME.

SHE DESCENDS RAPIDLY, AND USING A COVERED APPROACH...

...TAKES HER PREY BY SURPRISE. THE GRIP OF HER DEADLY TALONS, KILLS THE RABBIT AT ONCE.

SHE COVERS THE PREY WITH HER WINGS. SHE IS NOT TRYING TO HIDE IT FROM ANYONE. IT'S A COMMON PRACTICE AMONG EAGLES TO COVER THE PREY WITH THEIR WINGS. LATER SHE CARRIES THE RABBIT TO THEIR EATING PLACE AND BOTH SHE AND HER MATE HAVE A GOOD FEED.

AFTER EATING THEY SCRATCH THEIR BEAKS CLEAN ON THE BARK OF A TREE. THIS SCRATCHING KEEPS THEIR BEAKS SHARP TOO.

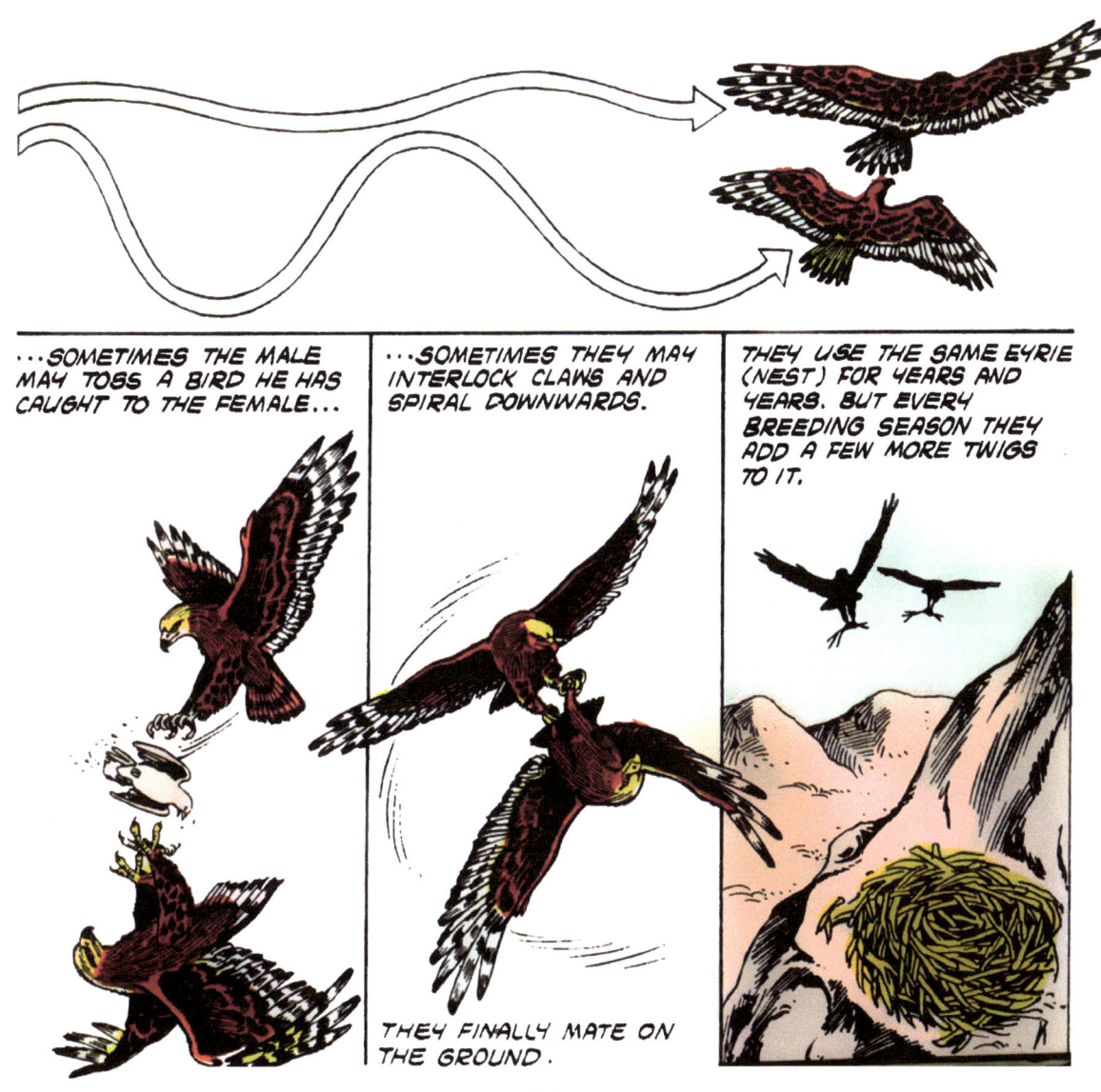

ABOUT 6 TO 8 HOURS AFTER THE MEAL, THEY THROW THE BONES AND FUR OR FEATHERS OF THEIR PREY OUT THROUGH THE MOUTH, IN THE FORM OF A PELLET.

AS WE SAW, GOLDEN EAGLES ARE GREAT HUNTERS. BUT WHEN FOOD IS SCARCE, THEY DON'T HESITATE TO FEED ON DEAD ANIMALS IN THE COMPANY OF VULTURES.

THESE PELLETS SHOULD NOT BE MISTAKEN FOR THEIR DROPPINGS.

IN LATE MARCH THEY MAY FLY IN A PECULIAR STYLE. IT'S THEIR BREEDING SEASON. BOTH OF THEM, BUT ESPECIALLY THE MALE, DO ACROBATICS IN THE AIR...

...SOMETIMES THE MALE MAY TOSS A BIRD HE HAS CAUGHT TO THE FEMALE...

...SOMETIMES THEY MAY INTERLOCK CLAWS AND SPIRAL DOWNWARDS.

THEY FINALLY MATE ON THE GROUND.

THEY USE THE SAME EYRIE (NEST) FOR YEARS AND YEARS. BUT EVERY BREEDING SEASON THEY ADD A FEW MORE TWIGS TO IT.

THE FEMALE LAYS TWO EGGS.

THEN SHE AND HER MATE PROCEED TO HATCH THEM. HOWEVER, IT IS THE FEMALE WHO SITS ON THE EGGS MOST OF THE TIME.

THE EGGS HATCH IN ABOUT 40 DAYS.

THE CHICKS ARE GLUTTONOUS. FOR THE FIRST FEW DAYS THEIR PARENTS PUT FOOD INTO THEIR MOUTHS...

BUT LATER THEY BRING HALF-DEAD PREY AND GIVE LESSONS TO THE YOUNG ONES ON HOW TO USE THEIR TALONS AND BEAKS.

THEN COME LESSONS IN FLYING AND HUNTING. THIS PERIOD (ABOUT A YEAR) IS A DIFFICULT ONE FOR YOUNG EAGLES.

ONCE THE TRAINING PERIOD IS OVER, THE YOUNG ONES LEAVE THEIR PARENTS AND THEIR TERRITORY. AND THE BOND BETWEEN THEM AND THEIR PARENTS IS BROKEN FOREVER.

IN OLDEN DAYS, SHEPHERDS OF CENTRAL ASIA USED TO KEEP TRAINED GOLDEN EAGLES.

THESE EAGLES WERE USED TO DRIVE AWAY WOLVES.

Result of the Complete-the-Story Competition held in the issue of June 5, 1983*

We received several hundred entries for the contest. The most popular ending had the Uncle coming out of the pond after some time and being mistaken for the Hippo. Afterwards the Uncle has to pay a fine or is informed that there is no Hippo in the pond. The entry we have selected for the first prize has an unusual twist to it at the end.

It was sent in by Swarna E. Kumar of Bangalore.

The prize-winning entry:

The little boy and the others kept looking at the spot where the Uncle had jumped in. Not seeing him anywhere in the pond, they all began to worry. All of a sudden, the man who was wearing the turban saw bubbles coming out of the water a little away from where the Uncle had jumped in. He began to shout: "There! There comes the Hippo!"

Everyone turned to look. They saw something shining and round in shape slowly rising up out of the water. The man in the turban cried out again: "Hey ... come out Fatso!" Soon everyone joined him in shouting: "Come on Fatso, come out so that we can see you!" But very soon they realised that the shining object was nothing but the head of the Uncle!

Uncle slowly came up and stood waist-deep in the water. He was dazed and so was the crowd. The crowd continued to shout: "Hey, Fatso, come out! Come out, you Fatso!" Just then, a Hippo slowly came out from the pond, close to Uncle! It looked at the crowd and turned its head towards Uncle. Both Uncle and the Hippo looked at each other for some time. Then the Hippo asked Uncle: "Who are they referring to? YOU or ME!!!"

* Refer to the footnote under the Editor's Note

Miss Swarna E. Kumar
C/o Sqn. Ldr. B. Ravi Kumar, 170/4, TRG Comd. Air Force, Hebbal, Bangalore 560 006.

A consolation prize of Rs. 25/- each has been awarded to Ravi Raman of Delhi and Sandeep Saterdekar of Goa.

NO. 41   Rs. 3

TINKLE

THE FORTNIGHTLY FOR CHILDREN FROM THE HOUSE OF AMAR CHITRA KATHA

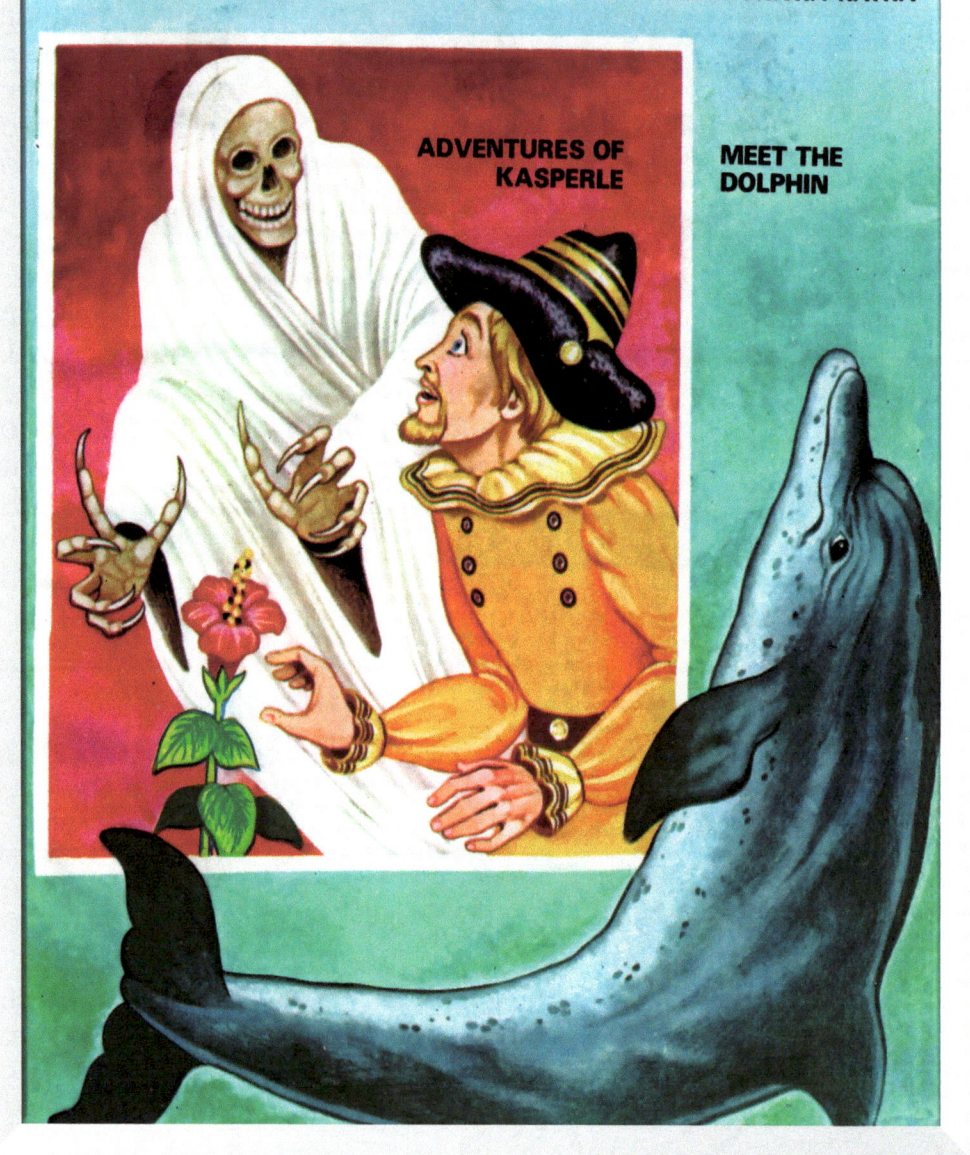

ADVENTURES OF KASPERLE

MEET THE DOLPHIN

ABOUT
SEE AND SMILE

As you flip through these pages, surely your eyes must have caught the small but hilarious one (or sometimes two) panel strip titled See and Smile. If you haven't seen it, go back and look for the pages where readers' letters, contests or subscription forms are printed. See and Smile was born on these pages.

Sometimes, the content for the above mentioned pages didn't quite fill the page. In such cases, to avoid noticeable white spaces, one to three panel gags were created. One of them was Mooshik, which featured a restless cat forever giving chase to a tiny mouse. The other was See and Smile. Mr. Vasant B. Halbe, a well-known artist and already an illustrator for *Tinkle*, illustrated the strip. (Keen readers might also recognize him as the original artist of Shikari Shambu!) The jokes in the strip focused on the various types of mischief children get up to. Mr. Halbe had a cartoony art style, which was perfectly suited for the cartoon-like hilarity of the strip.

See and Smile became so popular with readers that they began sending their ideas for it. In fact, artist Mr. Savio Mascarenhas, the current Art Director of *Tinkle* and *Amar Chitra Katha*, credits the strip for kick-starting his career in *Tinkle*. In the early 1990s, Mr. Mascarenhas was in the midst of his postgraduate studies when he sent some illustrated jokes to *Tinkle*. Mr. Anant Pai, the founder-editor of *Tinkle*, liked them so much that he asked Mr. Mascarenhas to take over the See and Smile strip. Thus began Mr. Mascarenhas' journey with *Tinkle*. His See and Smiles were such a hit that they became full-page jokes on the inside covers of *Tinkle Digest* and *Double Digest*.

From being a mere page filler to a career-making avenue, See and Smile has been on quite a transformative journey indeed.

Nasruddin Hodja

Script : Shruti Desai
Illustrations: Ram Waeerkar

YES, YES, WE KNOW WHAT YOU ARE GOING TO TALK ABOUT.
YOU DO?
THEN IN THAT CASE, IT WOULD BE A WASTE OF TIME TO SAY ANYTHING MORE, WOULDN'T IT?
BUT ONCE AGAIN—
NO, NO, HODJA. PLEASE GO BACK AND SAY A FEW WORDS TO THEM.
ALL RIGHT.
NOW BE PREPARED. DON'T LET HIM FOOL US A THIRD TIME.
WELL, HERE WE ARE AGAIN. DOES ANYBODY KNOW WHAT I AM GOING TO TALK ABOUT?
YES WE DO...
...I MEAN, SOME OF US DO AND SOME OF US DON'T.
WHAT A CLEVER ANSWER.
THEN IN THAT CASE, THOSE OF YOU WHO DO SHOULD INSTRUCT THOSE OF YOU WHO DON'T!
AND WITH THAT, THE HODJA WALKED AWAY... AND NOBODY TRIED TO STOP HIM THIS TIME.

EDITOR'S CHOICE

This story has been sent in by Ujwala V. Dalvi of Bombay

My young friends,
One day the moon felt very hungry and so he asked his mother for sugar balls, his favourite food. His mother gave him a bowlful. When her back was turned he took another bowlful and went and sat on a cloud to eat them.

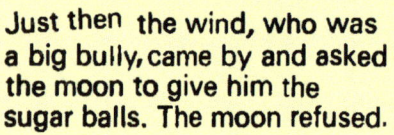

Just then the wind, who was a big bully, came by and asked the moon to give him the sugar balls. The moon refused.

At this, the wind got very angry and with a huff and puff he blew all the sugar balls away. The moon hurriedly got a lantern and set out to gather his precious sugar balls. But as soon as he got near them, the wind blew them further away. This happened again and again.

The moon is still chasing his sugar balls. The stars we see today are the sugar balls scattered over the sky. You can see them twinkling in the light of the moon's lantern.

Yours affectionately,
Uncle Pai

Mooshik
From an idea suggested by Dickey Das, Coimbatore

To Our Readers*

TINKLE SUBSCRIPTIONS :
All new subscriptions and renewals of the old ones are accepted at :

PARTHA BOOKS DIVISION
Nav Prabhat Chambers, Ranade Road, Dadar, Bombay 400 028.
The annual subscription rate for 24 issues is Rs. 72/- per year (add Rs. 3/- on outstation cheques). Drafts/cheques/M.O. should be in favour of PARTHA BOOKS DIVISION.

Readers' Contributions should be addressed to Editor, TINKLE, Mahalaxmi Chambers (Basement), 22 Bhulabhai Desai Road, Bombay 400 026.

Mooshik :
Rs. 10/- will pe paid for every original idea accepted.

Readers' Choice :
* Please send only folktales you have heard and not those you have read in books, magazines or textbooks. Rs. 25/- will be paid for every accepted contribution.
* Send a self-addressed stamped envelope if you want the story to be returned.
* Please do not send photographs until asked for.

This happened to me :
You can write on your own strange, thrilling or amusing experience or adventure. Rs. 15/- will be paid for every accepted contribution.

Readers Write...
1. Mail your letters to: Tinkle, P. Bag No. 16541, Bombay 400 026.
2. Please give your address in your letters, if you want a reply.

TINKLE TRICKS AND TREATS
1. Mail your entry to : Tinkle Competition Section, P. Bag No. 16541, Bombay 400 026.
2. The first 50 all-correct entries received by us will each win a set of personal letterheads, with the winners' names and addresses printed on them !
3. The next 350 all-correct entries received by us will each win a copy of the AMAR INDIA WALL PAPER No.18 dated October 1983

* Refer to the footnote under the Editor's Note

------------------------- CUT HERE

ENTRY FORM*   **MY SOLUTIONS**   **TTT-34**

NAME : _____

A _____

ADDRESS : _____

B _____

_____

C _____

STATE : _____

Tinkle Tricks & Treats* TTT-34

A Look again! Can you identify these objects?

1.
2.
3.

B Match the houses with the landscapes.

1. 2. 3. 4.
A. B. C. D.

C What is wrong here?

* Refer to the footnote under the Editor's Note

SOLUTIONS OF TTT—34

A—1. Shuttle cock 2. Book 3. Spectacles

B-1-D, 2-C, 3-A, 4-B

C—Its wheels are visible — which is a glaring error — as they lift into the plane's understructure during flight and only appear before landing.

69

Make your own COLOURFUL PUPPETS

You will need:
1. Round pots.
2. Coloured flowered cloth — about 1 foot wide and 2 feet long, for each pot.
3. Paint and brush to paint in eyes, nose, mouth, hair.

First of all, paint faces on the upside down pots — faces of men with moustaches, women with earrings, plaits etc. Let the pots dry.

Gather up the cloth and tie it around the neck of the pot. Your puppet is ready

Put your hand into the pot from under the cloth and it will move as your hand moves. You can even 'lend' your voice to it.

PUPPET SHOW

If you and your friends can get together, you can even have a puppet show.

Cover a table with a large cloth to hide its legs. Squat so that the audience cannot see you from the other side of the table.

Now try to tell a simple story with the help of the puppets. Speak for each of the puppets in a different voice.

See and Smile

Readers Write...

I got TINKLE No. 34 yesterday. The stories of "Kalia" and "The Goat and the Dog" were good. The very first story was really absurd and abnormal. The stories "Donkey and the Wolf" and "Gopal the Jester" are very common. You are publishing too many advertisements. There is not much attraction left in TINKLE. I do not think that you will publish this letter in "Readers Write" because I am not able to say anything good about your comic.

Soumya Ghosh
New Delhi

Could you please print more about science ? The language is so simple that even small children can understand such features and they help many of us at school.

V. Anuradha
New Delhi

Whenever I read comics my parents used to scold me. But to my surprise when they saw a TINKLE copy, they advised me to read this magazine regularly ! HURRAH ! Three cheers for TINKLE ! ! !

Semin Benazir
Gauhati

Mooshik

From an idea suggested by Ben Herold, Vizag.

The Tiger, The Bear And The Man

Story: J. S. Iyer
Illustrations: Ashok Dongre

A MAN WAS PASSING THROUGH A FOREST ONE EVENING WHEN—

A TIGER!

YIEEE!

GROWL!

GROWL!

!!

BROTHER BEAR, PLEASE PUSH THAT HUMAN DOWN. HE IS AN INTRUDER IN OUR WORLD AND HE IS VERY SELFISH.

I CAN'T, BROTHER TIGER. THIS IS MY HOME AND HE IS MY GUEST.
SLEEP NOW. BY DAWN THE TIGER WILL GO AWAY AND YOU CAN GET DOWN.
THE TIGER WAITED TILL THE BEAR WAS ASLEEP. THEN—
YOU ARE A STUPID MAN! THE BEAR IS CERTAIN TO KILL YOU. WHY DON'T YOU PUSH HIM DOWN...
... AND I WILL EAT HIM INSTEAD.
HE IS RIGHT. THE BEAR IS NOT HUNGRY NOW, BUT HE WILL BE WHEN HE WAKES UP.
I WILL PUSH HIM DOWN.

WHACK

"THE TIGER WAS RIGHT. YOU HUMANS ARE VERY SELFISH..."

"...BUT I STILL WON'T HARM YOU AS YOU ARE MY GUEST."

"OH DEAR! WHAT A WASTE OF TIME! THERE'S NOTHING HERE FOR ME."

AT DAWN—

"GET OFF MY TREE! AND GO AWAY!"

THE MAN, ASHAMED OF HIMSELF, CLIMBED DOWN...

...AND WENT AWAY.

THE BOY AND HIS COINS

Illustrations: Ram Waeerkar

Based on a story sent by S. Prema, Arcot

Anand used to make a living by selling wood. One day—

"This load is very heavy."

"But it will fetch me a lot of money."

And sure enough—

"Young man, you must not count money in the open. Someone may steal it from you."

"?"

"You look tired and hungry. Come, I will give you something to eat."

"Thank you, kind lady. Food would be most welcome."

Some time later—

"No more... I am full!"

I'LL TAKE A STROLL THROUGH THE TOWN BEFORE I GO HOME.
A WORD OF WARNING, SON. THERE ARE PICKPOCKETS IN THE TOWN...
WHY DON'T YOU KEEP YOUR MONEY WITH ME? YOU CAN COLLECT IT ON YOUR WAY HOME.
YES, I'LL DO THAT.
HERE.
THE HOUSES LOOK SO SIMILAR! HOW WILL I FIND YOUR HOUSE IN THE DARK?
I'LL KEEP A LAMP OUTSIDE THE DOOR.
WHAT A KIND LADY SHE IS...
BUT WHEN THE BOY RETURNED IN THE EVENING —
THERE'S NO LAMP OUTSIDE ANY DOOR. NOW HOW WILL I FIND HER HOUSE?
I HAVE BEEN TRICKED! SHE WAS AFTER MY MONEY.

THE BOY BEGAN TO CRY...
AND SOON A CROWD COLLECTED...
WHAT'S THE MATTER, BOY?
LOST YOUR WAY?
DON'T CRY!
I FOUND TEN GOLD COINS ON THE ROAD.
AND I WANT TO KEEP THEM WITH THE KIND LADY WHO HELPED ME, BUT I CAN'T FIND HER HOUSE!
HERE I AM, BOY. HERE I AM! GIVE ME THE COINS!
THE ONLY COINS I HAD ARE WITH YOU.
NOW MAY I HAVE THEM BACK?
TRICKED!
THE OLD WOMAN COULD DO NOTHING ELSE BUT RETURN THE BOY'S MONEY.

THE MOON — Our strange neighbour — 3

Script: J.D. Isloor • Illustrations: Anand Mande

THE MOON GOES ROUND THE EARTH. IT MOVES VERY FAST, COVERING ABOUT 60,000 KM. PER DAY.
YET IT TAKES 27 1/3 DAYS TO CIRCLE THE EARTH ONCE. AS IT GOES ROUND THE EARTH, IT ALSO SPINS LIKE A TOP.
A TOP SPINS VERY FAST. IT TAKES NO TIME AT ALL TO MAKE ONE TURN. BUT THE MOON SPINS VERY SLOWLY IN COMPARISON. IT TAKES 27 1/3 DAYS TO MAKE ONE TURN. YOU WILL NOTICE THAT IT TAKES THE SAME NUMBER OF DAYS TO TURN ONCE ROUND ITSELF AND TO MAKE ONE ORBIT ROUND THE EARTH.

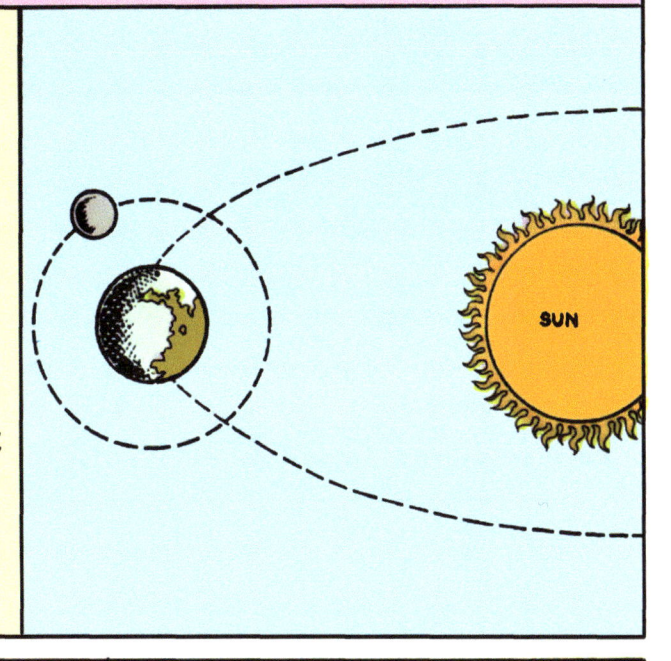

IF YOU KEEP A CHAIR IN THE CENTRE OF A ROOM AND GO ROUND IT IN AN ANTI-CLOCKWISE DIRECTION, IT IS YOUR LEFT SIDE WHICH WILL BE TURNED TOWARDS IT ALL THE TIME.

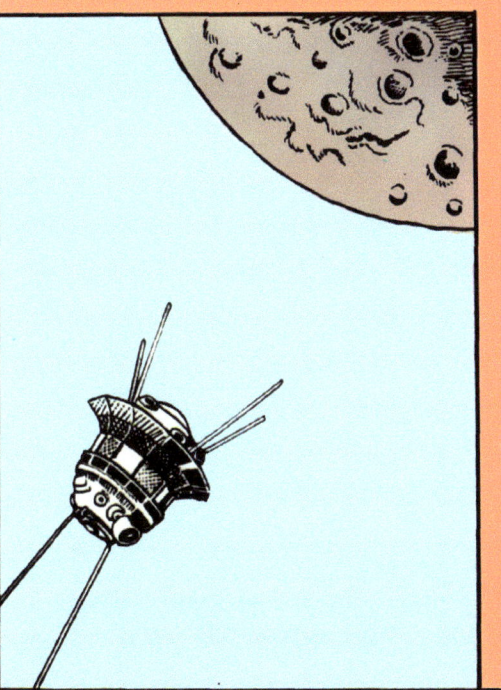

SIMILARLY, AS THE MOON TRAVELS ROUND THE EARTH, IT KEEPS THE SAME SIDE TURNED TOWARDS THE EARTH. WHEN GALILEO LOOKED AT THE MOON THROUGH HIS TELESCOPE, IT WAS THIS SIDE THAT HE SAW.
NOBODY KNEW WHAT THE HIDDEN SIDE OF THE MOON LOOKED LIKE UNTIL 1959. IN THAT YEAR THE RUSSIAN SPACECRAFT, LUNA 3, PASSED BEHIND THE MOON, TOOK PICTURES AND SENT THEM BACK TO EARTH.
IT WAS FOUND THAT THE HIDDEN SIDE LOOKED VERY MUCH LIKE THE SIDE TURNED TOWARDS US.

HAVE A LOOK AT THE FRIENDLY FACE OF THE MOON (SIDE FACING US). THERE ARE PLACES WITH NAMES LIKE SEA OF CLOUDS (MARE NUBIUM), SEA OF NECTAR (MARE NECTAR) AND SEA OF RAINS (MARE INTRIUM). ACTUALLY THERE ARE NO SEAS OR RIVERS OR PONDS ON THE MOON. IN FACT, THERE IS NOT A DROP OF WATER THERE.
THE SEAS MENTIONED ARE FAIRLY SMOOTH PLAINS.

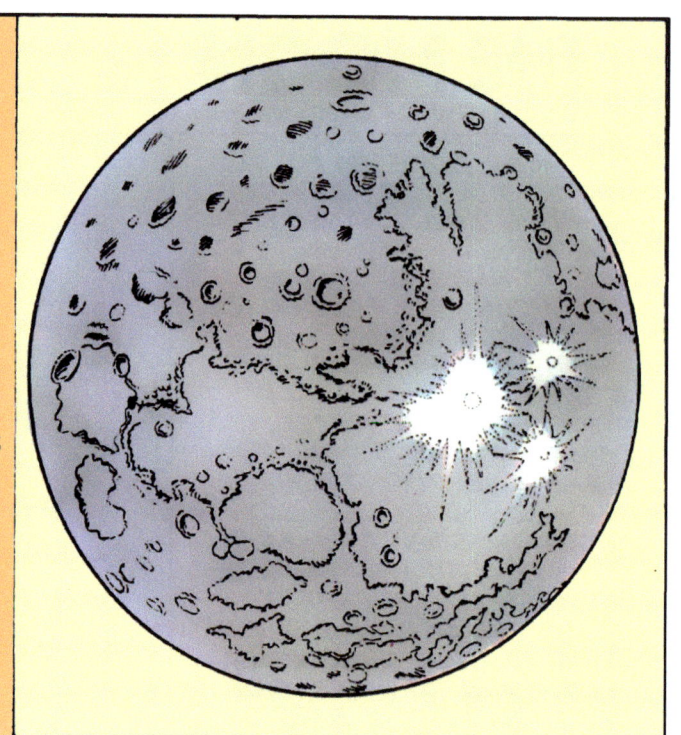

JUST AS THE MOON TRAVELS ROUND THE EARTH, THE EARTH TRAVELS ROUND THE SUN.
ONCE A MONTH, THE SUN, EARTH AND MOON ARE IN THIS POSITION—

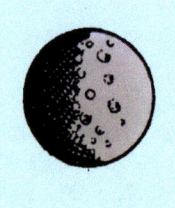

EARTH   MOON   SUN

THE SIDE OF THE MOON TURNED TOWARDS THE EARTH IS NOT LIGHTED UP BY THE SUN AND SO WE CAN'T SEE THE MOON AT ALL. WE SAY IT IS A NEW MOON.

TWO WEEKS LATER, THE SUN, THE EARTH AND THE MOON ARE IN THIS POSITION —

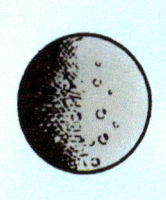

THEN THE SUN CAN SHINE ON THE SIDE OF THE MOON WHICH IS TOWARDS US AND WE SEE A FULL MOON.

ANOTHER TWO WEEKS AND THE THREE BODIES ARE BACK IN THE FIRST POSITION. IN BETWEEN, SOME BUT NOT ALL OF THE MOON'S LIGHTED SIDE IS TURNED TOWARDS US AND WE SEE THE MOON BECOMING EITHER FULLER AND FULLER OR THINNER AND THINNER.

SO EVEN THOUGH ONE HALF OF THE MOON IS ALWAYS LIGHTED BY THE SUN, WE CAN SEE THE FULL LIGHTED SIDE OF THE MOON ONLY ONCE A MONTH. THE REST OF THE TIME WE CAN SEE ONLY PARTS OF THE LIGHTED SIDE AND AT NEW MOON WE CAN'T SEE IT AT ALL.
IF WE WERE WATCHING OUR EARTH FROM THE MOON WE WOULD SEE OUR EARTH TOO IN VARIOUS SHAPES AND SIZES.

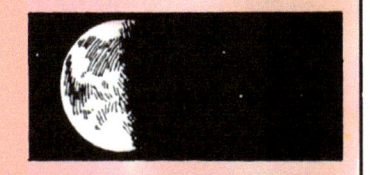

PHASES OF THE MOON

The Face in the Window

Readers' Choice — Illustrations: Ram Waeerkar
Based on a story sent by Tanuj Kumar, New Delhi

ONE DAY A MAN WENT TO THE HOUSE OF HIS FRIEND, A RICH MERCHANT.

YES?

I HAD ASKED YOUR MASTER FOR A LOAN AND HE CALLED ME TODAY. PLEASE TELL HIM I'VE COME.

I'M SORRY. THE MASTER HAS GONE OUT.

HAS HE?

TELL HIM THAT THE NEXT TIME HE GOES OUT...

...HE SHOULD TAKE HIS FACE ALONG WITH HIM AND NOT LEAVE IT IN THE WINDOW!

Kalia
THE CROW
Script:
LUIS
Illustrations:
PRADEEP SATHE
KEECHU AND MEECHU SAID THEY WOULD MEET ME HERE. I'M EARLY I GUESS...
...OH-OH, HERE COMES TROUBLE.
YOU SEE THAT LOG?
YES... WHAT ABOUT IT?
IT'S HOLLOW... HEE HEE.
IT'S A GOOD HIDING PLACE, CHAMATAKA.
YES. AND THERE'S LOTS OF ROOM HERE.
I DON'T HAVE TO CROUCH.
THAT'S NOT SURPRISING...
...YOU'RE VERY SHORT YOU KNOW.

ER ... IS THERE ANYTHING YOU WANT ME TO DO?
YES. HIDE IN THAT GRASS AND GRUNT WHEN YOU SEE AN ANIMAL APPROACHING.
IF THEY PULL THIS OFF, MY FRIENDS AND I WILL NEVER BE ABLE TO USE THIS AS A MEETING PLACE AGAIN.
THEY'LL ALWAYS BE HANGING AROUND HERE.
DOOB-DOOB, WHAT ARE YOU DOING THERE?
HIDING.
I ... I MEAN, NOTHING.
I HEARD CHAMATAKA TELLING YOU TO GRUNT WHEN AN ANIMAL COMES BY.
WELL, HERE COMES ONE.
I CAN SEE AS WELL AS YOU. YOU DON'T HAVE TO TELL ME WHAT TO DO.

GROOT! GROOT!
THE SIGNAL!
AAAAAH!
SPLOT!
SOMETHING HAS GONE WRONG.
THAT IDIOT CHAMATAKA NEVER GIVES CLEAR INSTRUCTIONS.
PERHAPS I SHOULD'VE WAITED FOR A SMALLER ANIMAL.
THEY'VE GONE... AND JUST IN TIME. HERE COME KEECHU AND MEECHU.

Readers' Choice

STONE SOUP

Illustrations : Ram Waeerkar

Based on a story sent by Philip Fernandes, Goa

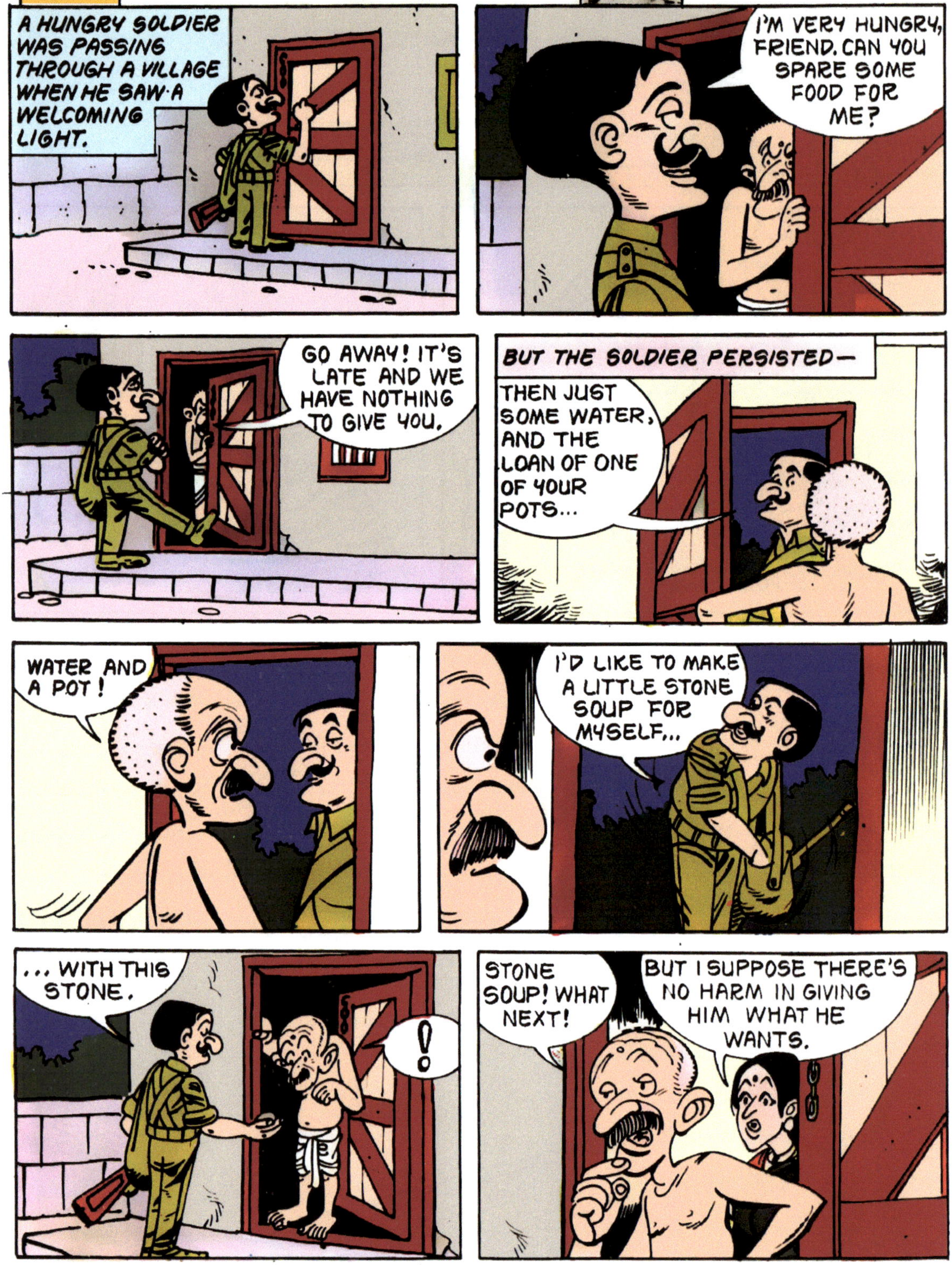

THANK YOU, GOOD LADY. WOULD YOU MIND VERY MUCH IF I KEPT THE POT ON YOUR FIRE?
OH, ALL RIGHT, IF YOU MUST. COME IN.
SHE PUT A POT OF WATER ON THE FIRE AND TOOK THE SOLDIER TO THE KITCHEN.
NOW I'LL PUT THIS STONE IN THE WATER AND WAIT FOR IT TO COOK.
THE FARMER AND HIS WIFE SAT BACK TO WATCH THE STRANGE COOK AT WORK.
A LITTLE LATER THE SOLDIER OPENED THE POT AND PEERED IN.
LET ME TASTE IT...
AH! IT'S COMING ALONG ...
... BUT IT NEEDS A BIT OF SALT.
WAIT, I'LL GET YOU SOME...
THE SOLDIER ADDED THE SALT.

AFTER SOME TIME —
I SHOULD TASTE IT AGAIN, DON'T YOU THINK?
THE FARMER WAS GETTING IMPATIENT.
YES, YES, BUT BE QUICK ABOUT IT!
IS IT VERY TASTY?
WELL, WELL!
IT IS! BUT WHAT WOULDN'T AN ONION DO TO IMPROVE THE TASTE!
WIFE, GO AND GET HIM AN ONION QUICKLY, OTHERWISE HE'LL BE HERE ALL NIGHT.
THE FARMER'S WIFE WENT OFF AND...
...SOON A CHOPPED ONION WAS ADDED TO THE SOUP.

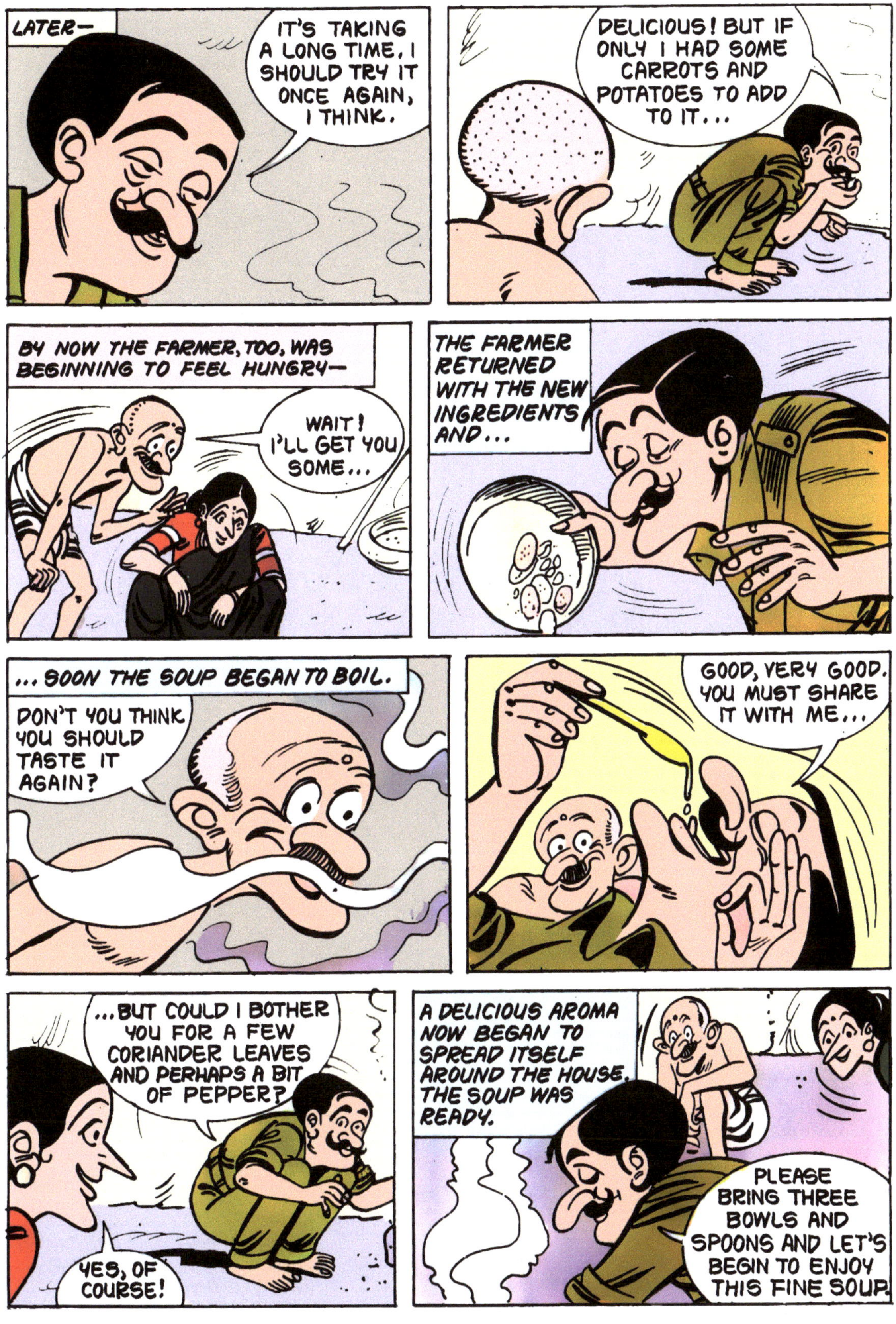
LATER—
IT'S TAKING A LONG TIME, I SHOULD TRY IT ONCE AGAIN, I THINK.
DELICIOUS! BUT IF ONLY I HAD SOME CARROTS AND POTATOES TO ADD TO IT...
BY NOW THE FARMER, TOO, WAS BEGINNING TO FEEL HUNGRY—
WAIT! I'LL GET YOU SOME...
THE FARMER RETURNED WITH THE NEW INGREDIENTS AND...
... SOON THE SOUP BEGAN TO BOIL.
DON'T YOU THINK YOU SHOULD TASTE IT AGAIN?
GOOD, VERY GOOD. YOU MUST SHARE IT WITH ME...
...BUT COULD I BOTHER YOU FOR A FEW CORIANDER LEAVES AND PERHAPS A BIT OF PEPPER?
YES, OF COURSE!
A DELICIOUS AROMA NOW BEGAN TO SPREAD ITSELF AROUND THE HOUSE. THE SOUP WAS READY.
PLEASE BRING THREE BOWLS AND SPOONS AND LET'S BEGIN TO ENJOY THIS FINE SOUP.

HERE IS SOME BREAD AS WELL.
FINALLY, THEY ALL SAT DOWN TO EAT.
IT'S DELICIOUS!
MMM, SO IT IS! HOW DID YOU DO IT?
ALL THANKS TO THIS STONE OF MINE.
MAY WE HAVE A CLOSER LOOK AT IT PLEASE?
I'M SORRY MY GOOD FRIENDS, BUT YOU MUST ALLOW ME MY LITTLE SECRET!
THANK YOU AND GOOD NIGHT!
AND THE SOLDIER WENT ON HIS WAY, HUNGRY NO LONGER.

THE CLEVER FARMER

Illustrations: Dilip Kadam

Readers' Choice

Based on a story sent by Trilok Singh Chandwani, Mandsaur

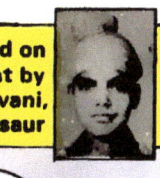

ONE EVENING A FARMER WAS RETURNING HOME FROM A FAIR.

SUDDENLY—

HALT!

GIVE ME EVERYTHING YOU HAVE!

OR I'LL KNOCK YOUR HEAD OFF.

NO! NO!

HERE, TAKE EVERYTHING.

THE BUFFALO TOO!

YOU HAVE TAKEN EVERYTHING. AT LEAST GIVE ME YOUR STICK. PLEASE.
WHY?
I MUST HAVE SOMETHING TO TAKE HOME TO MY WIFE.
AH, WELL...
...TAKE IT! AND GOODBYE.
NOT SO SOON, FRIEND!
I WANT EVERYTHING BACK!
C-CERTAINLY!
H-HERE, TAKE EVERYTHING.
THE ROBBER RAN AWAY. AND THE FARMER HAD NO MORE TROUBLE ALONG THE WAY.

The Baby Elephant

Illustrations: M. Mohandas

Readers' Choice — Based on a story sent by D. Ramesh Kumar, Vetapalem

ELEPHANTS AT ONE TIME HAD SMALL TRUNKS. ONE DAY A BABY ELEPHANT WAS WALKING NEAR A SWAMP...

...AND HE SAW A CROCODILE COMING OUT OF THE RIVER.

"THESE ANIMALS SPEND ALL THEIR TIME IN THE WATER."

"I WONDER WHAT THEY EAT?"

"WHAT DO YOU EAT, UNCLE CROCODILE?"

"EAT?"

"I EAT MANY THINGS..."

"...INCLUDING ELEPHANTS."

?!

"LET ME GO!"

"HELP! HELP!"

"HELP!"

"LET HIM GO, YOU BIG BULLY!"

THE PYTHON WRAPPED THE LOWER HALF OF HIS BODY ROUND THE ELEPHANT...

...AND TRIED TO PULL HIM AWAY FROM THE CROCODILE.

THE TUG-OF-WAR WENT ON FOR A LONG TIME.

FINALLY—

DON'T CRY. YOU'RE SAFE NOW.

YES.

BUT LOOK AT MY TRUNK! IT'S BECOME SO LONG.

A LONG TRUNK COULD BE VERY USEFUL.

THE PYTHON WAS RIGHT. ALL ELEPHANTS TODAY HAVE LONG TRUNKS. AND THEIR TRUNKS ARE VERY, VERY USEFUL TO THEM.

NO. 43   Rs. 3

TINKLE

THE FORTNIGHTLY FOR CHILDREN FROM THE HOUSE OF AMAR CHITRA KATHA

THE DWARF AND THE GIANT

MEET THE SPIDER

THE BABY ELEPHANT

SAY HELLO TO

> HE'S RIGHT. WE WILL AVOID THAT ROUTE. HULIA CAN'T DO A THING.

K. CHANDRANATH

Of the many brilliant artists in our country, a shining name is that of Mr. K. Chandranath. Even today Mr. Chandranath remains one of the most renowned artists from Karnataka.

When Mr. Subba Rao (co-founder of *Tinkle*) first laid eyes on Mr. Chandranath's work, he immediately thought him perfect for an *Amar Chitra Katha* book, *Hukka Bukka*— based on the mighty rulers of Vijaynagar in Southern India.

Getting Mr. Chandranath to illustrate this book was no easy task. Back then, he was an extremely busy man. He dabbled in various art forms, from photography to oil paintings. Despite juggling multiple projects, Mr. Chandranath decided to make time for the book. He took about three years to complete the 32-page book. It may have taken a while but *Hukka Bukka* remains memorable to this day.

Mr. Chandranath wasn't an artist who would mindlessly illustrate a story. He is known as a thinking artist. His love for learning was such that between his pressing commitments and while he was still working on *Hukka Bukka*, he enrolled himself in the Shanti Niketan School of Arts, Kolkata.

After *Hukka Bukka*, Mr. Chanrdranath started illustrating shorter stories for *Tinkle* such as 'Punyakoti' and 'The Treasure Hunt'. These stories, like their artist, hold a special place in *Tinkle*'s history.

MEET THE SPIDER

Script: Ashvin
Illustrations: Pradeep Sathe

You must have seen spider webs. But have you seen the great weaver of the web at close range?

Here it is! Looking at you with its eight eyes. Yes, eight!

It has eight legs too! Long, hairy legs.....

It has arms of a sort...

...and two sharp fangs connected to poison glands.

Although closely related to the insect family, the spider is not an insect. Its body is divided into two parts — head and abdomen.

SPIDER

HONEY-BEE — AN INSECT

An insect's body is divided into three parts and they have six legs.

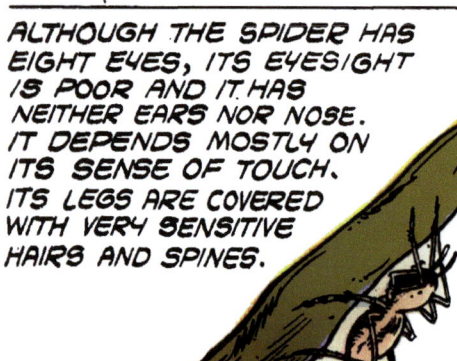

Although the spider has eight eyes, its eyesight is poor and it has neither ears nor nose. It depends mostly on its sense of touch. Its legs are covered with very sensitive hairs and spines.

Let's watch this young male spin a web. He drops down from a branch, pressing out a silky thread from the end of his his abdomen.

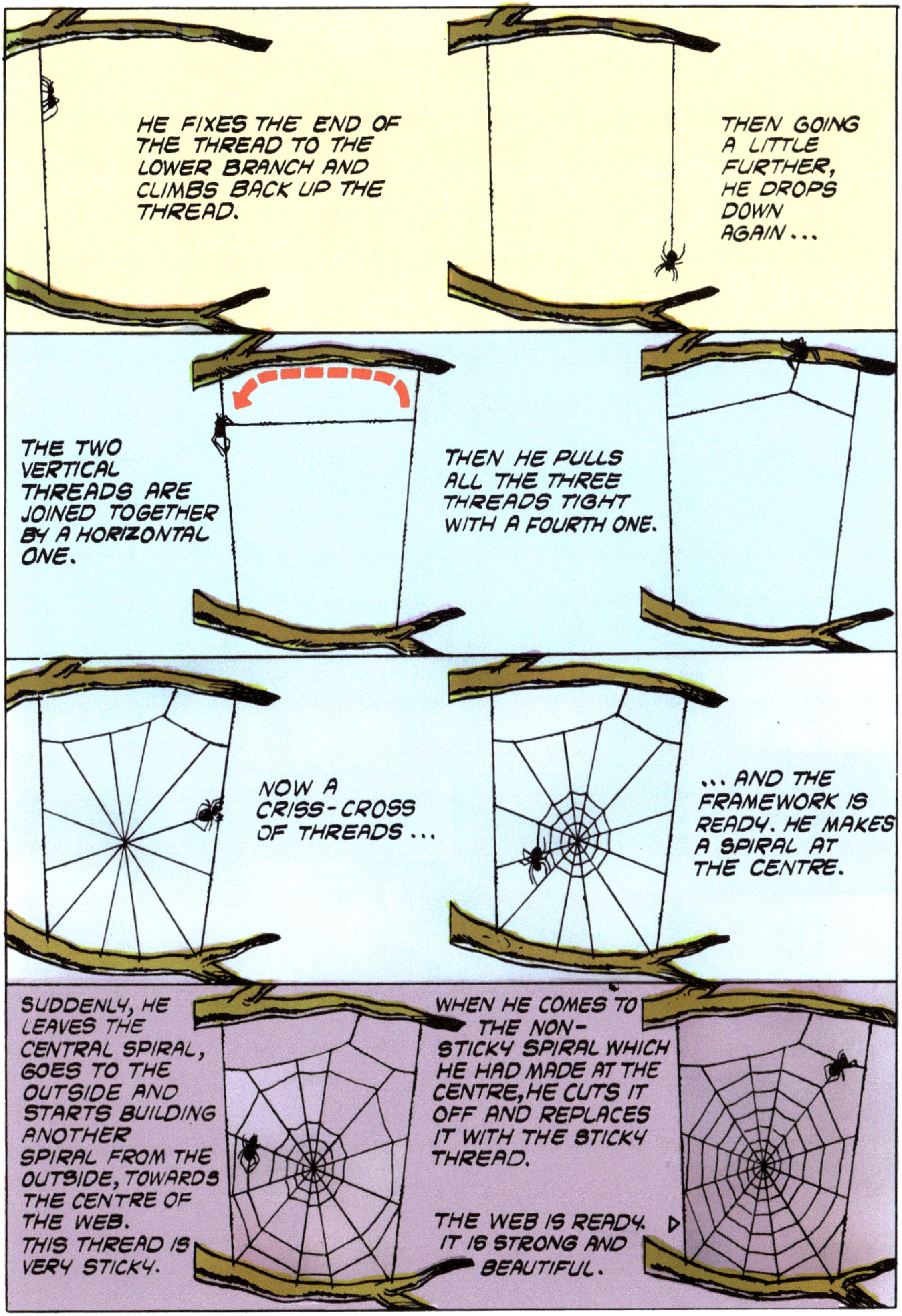
HE FIXES THE END OF THE THREAD TO THE LOWER BRANCH AND CLIMBS BACK UP THE THREAD.
THEN GOING A LITTLE FURTHER, HE DROPS DOWN AGAIN ...
THE TWO VERTICAL THREADS ARE JOINED TOGETHER BY A HORIZONTAL ONE.
THEN HE PULLS ALL THE THREE THREADS TIGHT WITH A FOURTH ONE.
NOW A CRISS-CROSS OF THREADS ...
... AND THE FRAMEWORK IS READY. HE MAKES A SPIRAL AT THE CENTRE.
SUDDENLY, HE LEAVES THE CENTRAL SPIRAL, GOES TO THE OUTSIDE AND STARTS BUILDING ANOTHER SPIRAL FROM THE OUTSIDE, TOWARDS THE CENTRE OF THE WEB. THIS THREAD IS VERY STICKY.
WHEN HE COMES TO THE NON-STICKY SPIRAL WHICH HE HAD MADE AT THE CENTRE, HE CUTS IT OFF AND REPLACES IT WITH THE STICKY THREAD.
THE WEB IS READY. IT IS STRONG AND BEAUTIFUL.

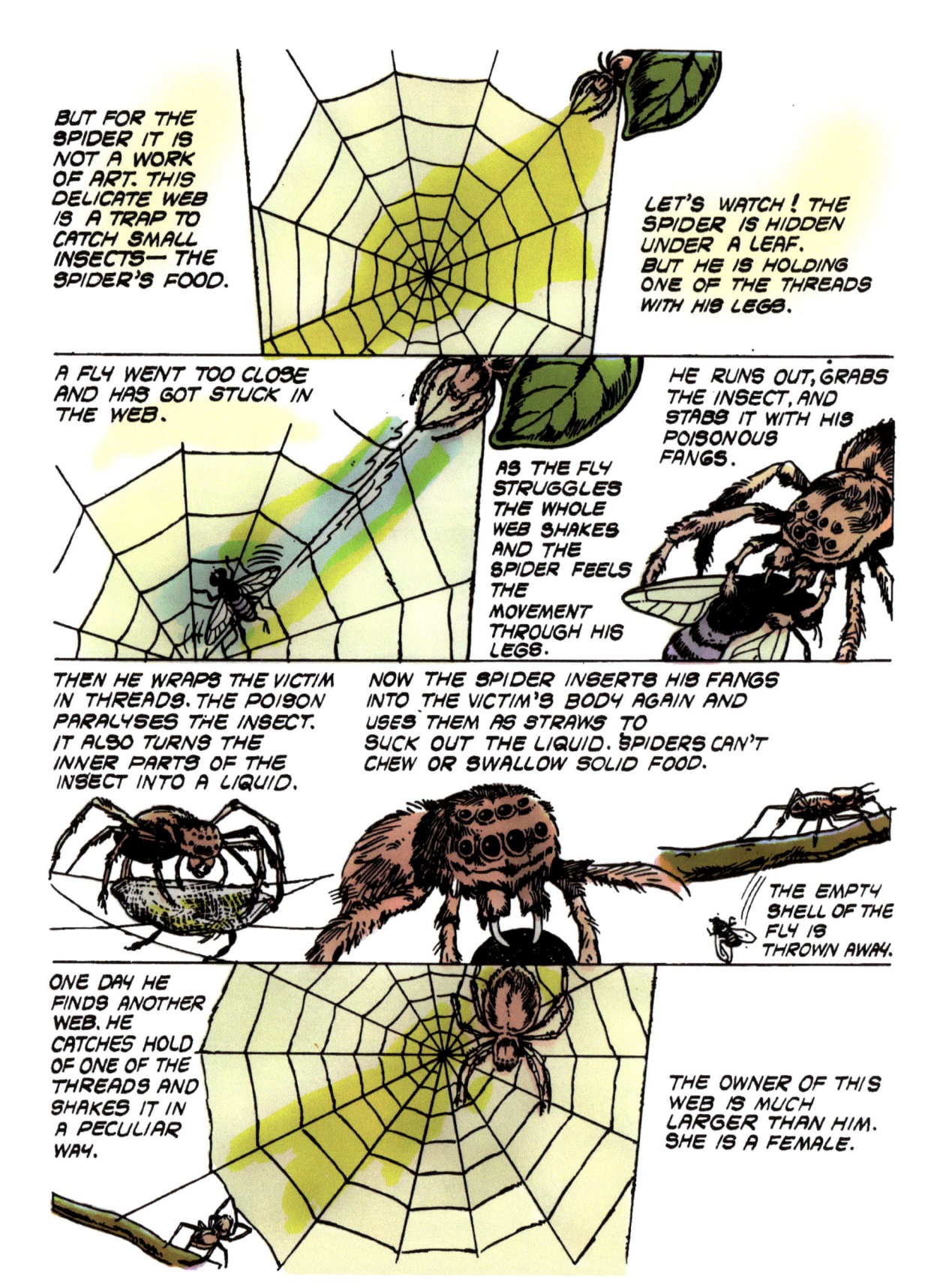

BUT FOR THE SPIDER IT IS NOT A WORK OF ART. THIS DELICATE WEB IS A TRAP TO CATCH SMALL INSECTS — THE SPIDER'S FOOD.

LET'S WATCH! THE SPIDER IS HIDDEN UNDER A LEAF. BUT HE IS HOLDING ONE OF THE THREADS WITH HIS LEGS.

A FLY WENT TOO CLOSE AND HAS GOT STUCK IN THE WEB.

AS THE FLY STRUGGLES THE WHOLE WEB SHAKES AND THE SPIDER FEELS THE MOVEMENT THROUGH HIS LEGS.

HE RUNS OUT, GRABS THE INSECT, AND STABS IT WITH HIS POISONOUS FANGS.

THEN HE WRAPS THE VICTIM IN THREADS. THE POISON PARALYSES THE INSECT. IT ALSO TURNS THE INNER PARTS OF THE INSECT INTO A LIQUID.

NOW THE SPIDER INSERTS HIS FANGS INTO THE VICTIM'S BODY AGAIN AND USES THEM AS STRAWS TO SUCK OUT THE LIQUID. SPIDERS CAN'T CHEW OR SWALLOW SOLID FOOD.

THE EMPTY SHELL OF THE FLY IS THROWN AWAY.

ONE DAY HE FINDS ANOTHER WEB. HE CATCHES HOLD OF ONE OF THE THREADS AND SHAKES IT IN A PECULIAR WAY.

THE OWNER OF THIS WEB IS MUCH LARGER THAN HIM. SHE IS A FEMALE.

The male goes up to her, holds her at a distance with his front legs and catches hold of her fangs, so that she can't bite him.

Then they mate. After mating the mate runs for his life.

About three months later the female lays her eggs in silken cocoons. Each cocoon holds around 600 eggs.

After some days the eggs hatch. As soon as the spiderlings (baby spiders) come out...

...they spin a mass of silken threads. It is their temporary home.

At this stage, males and females are of equal size, but females grow rapidly and become larger. Spiders grow by molting. They molt about 8 to 12 times and within a year they become adults.

You have just met the garden spider. There are some 40,000 species of spiders. Almost all of them spin webs (though the patterns are different). Some species have fewer eyes.

THE NEPHILA

It is a large species of garden spider found in southeast Asia. It spins a giant web, which may be as much as 2·4 metres across, between trees. The thread is so thick and tough that the local people use these webs as fishing nets.

THE HOUSE-SPIDER

It is smaller in size than the garden spider. It spins an irregular web.

THE TARANTULA

The largest spider. It has a leg span of 25 cm.

THE BLACK WIDOW

The females of this species are dangerously poisonous.

MALE   FEMALE

ANWAR
by
Appaswami
Illustrations: V. B. Halbe
AMMA, WHERE DO FROGS COME FROM?
DO THEY DROP DOWN FROM ABOVE WHEN IT RAINS?
COME, I'LL TELL YOU HOW A FROG IS BORN.
LOOK. THIS IS A TADPOLE...
THIS IS HOW IT... IT...
YES AMMA?
IT... THAT... TOWEL... IS JUMPING...
?
OH!
YEEE!
MY PET!
IT'S GONE.
AMMA, YOU WERE TELLING ME ABOUT TADPOLES...
ANWAR, DON'T MENTION TADPOLES AGAIN, I BEG YOU.

DID YOU KNOW?

THE YETI

The Sherpas of Nepal believe that man-like creatures called Yetis roam the lower slopes of the Himalayas.

Several other people besides the Sherpas say they've seen the strange creatures. These eye-witnesses say that the creatures are huge and hairy

But though their footprints have been photographed, no one has been able to get a picture of the creatures themselves.

Some scientists say there is no such thing as a Yeti. They say that the people who claim to have seen them were just imagining things.

They say the tracks in the snow are made by bears or large monkeys.

Other scientists say the Yetis are a very old race of men.

Another name for the Yeti is the 'Abominable Snowman'.

SAY IT YOURSELF* AND WIN A CASH PRIZE — NO. 3

ARE YOU HURT?

WHAT DO YOU THINK THE BOY IS SAYING?

* Refer to the footnote under the Editor's Note

1. Mail your entry to:
   TINKLE
   Competition Section,
   P. Bag No. 16541
   Bombay 400 026

2.
   - First prize — Rs. 50/-
   - Second prize — Rs. 25/-
   - Third prize — Rs. 15/-
   - 10 Consolation prizes, — Rs. 10/- each

3. Decision of the judges is final and binding. Names of the prize-winners will be announced in TINKLE No. 47 dated 20th November 1983

Last date for receiving entries: October 10, 1983

ENTRY FORM*　　　　　　　　　　　Say it Yourself – 3

NAME _____　　Answer: _____

ADDRESS _____　　_____

_____　　_____

STATE _____

PIN _____ ☐☐☐☐☐☐

RESULTS OF SAY IT YOURSELF* No.1

FIRST PRIZE: (Rs. 50)
Niti Vasant Ashar
9, Bhatia Building,
S.V. Road, Vile Parle West, Bombay 400 056.

SECOND PRIZE: (Rs. 25)
Ninad A. Kamat
D-10, Gayatri Apts, Mahadevbhai Desai Road,
Borivli East, Bombay 400 066.

THIRD PRIZE: (Rs. 15)
Puja Palta
14, Pushp Vilas 338, Chimbai Road,
Bandra, Bombay 400 050.

CONSOLATION PRIZES of Rs. 10 each

Manish Assudani Ahmedabad	**G. V. Anand** Bombay
Venkat Kini Bombay	**Pankaj Kumar Dodeja** Baroda
Tusheel Bhatt Bombay	**Jyoti Cardoza** Bombay
Rajesh M. Bhatia Bombay	**Rohit S. Parelkar** Bombay
Manoj Gopinathan Bombay	**K. Tulsi Iyer** Bombay

YOU'RE READING ABOUT KANGAROOS!

Sir! I was trying to make you happy by doing further studies.

PRIZE-WINNING ENTRY FROM NITI VASANT ASHAR

* Refer to the footnote under the Editor's Note

Mooshik
Based on an idea suggested by C. Venkateshwara Rao, Hyderabad

NAVRANG DYERS

EDITOR'S CHOICE

Azra Fathima

My young friends,

This fortnight I have chosen a story written by Kumari Azra Fathima of Bangalore.

Once an old sage sat meditating under a banyan tree. He was blind.

A man came up and said: "Hey! old man, did you hear anyone passing this way?" The sage replied, "No, my good man, I did not hear anyone."

After a while another man went up to the old sage and asked, "Old man, did you hear anyone going this way?" The sage replied, "Oh yes, a man went by just now and he asked the same question." The man went away.

After some time another man came and asked, "Noble sir, did you hear anyone passing this way?"

The old sage replied, "Yes, Your Majesty. A soldier went first and then your chief minister. Both of them asked the same question." The man was surprised and asked, "Good sir, how do you know that I am a king and that the other two were a soldier and a chief minister?"

The sage answered, "Your Majesty, I knew them by their manner of speaking. The first man spoke very rudely. The second was a little more polite, but Your Majesty was the most polite."

The king went away astonished at the sage's astuteness.

Affectionately yours,

Uncle Pai

A Friend in Need
By Pradeep Sathe
A prince was being pursued by his enemies.
That spider could save my life.

Sometime later—
Where could he have gone?
He may be hiding in that cave.
Can't you see there's a cobweb covering the entrance?
It would have broken if anyone had gone through it.
You're right!
Let's go! He's not here!
Saved! You've saved my life, my little friend.

SEARCHING FOR SUNKEN TREASURE

Script: Padmini Rao Banerjee
Illustrations: Pradeep Sathe

OVER THE CENTURIES, MANY SHIPS HAVE SET SAIL FOR OTHER LANDS CARRYING GOLD, SILVER AND PRECIOUS GEMS, ALONG THE OLD TRADE ROUTES.

SOME OF THESE SHIPS NEVER REACHED THEIR DESTINATIONS.

SOME LOST THEIR WAY DURING A STORM AT SEA AND WERE NEVER HEARD OF AGAIN...

...OTHERS RAN AGROUND ON REEFS IN THE MIDDLE OF THE SEA...

...AND SANK TO THE BOTTOM.

AS THE WRECKS SETTLED, THE TREASURE THEY HELD SCATTERED ALL OVER THE SEA-FLOOR.

WHAT A TREASURE LIES HERE — A FORTUNE READY TO BE PICKED UP BY ANYONE WHO TRIES HARD ENOUGH...

DIVING FOR TREASURE IS AN OLD, OLD SKILL. IN THE OLD DAYS WHENEVER A CARGO OF TREASURE WAS LOST AT A KNOWN SPOT, MEN DIVED IN TO RECOVER IT BEFORE IT SANK OUT OF REACH.

BUT MUCH OF THE WORLD'S TREASURE STILL LIES UNDISCOVERED. THE SEA IS VAST AND DEEP. AS WE GO DEEPER, THE PRESSURE OF THE WATER UPON OUR BODIES INCREASES.

BEYOND A POINT, THE PRESSURE CAN EVEN CRUSH A MAN TO DEATH.

DIVING EQUIPMENT HAS IMPROVED A GREAT DEAL OVER THE CENTURIES.

HERE IS A PRESENT-DAY TREASURE-HUNTER SEARCHING NEAR AN OLD WRECK.

AH! HE HAS FOUND SOMETHING!

...FLATTISH BLACK DISCS! THEY ARE CURRENCY COINS OF SILVER, NOW DISCOLOURED.

THEY ARE ALL STUCK TOGETHER, AS IF IN A LUMP.

THE TREASURE IS HAULED UP WITH A ROPE.

Sometimes a cargo of treasure may be so heavy that an inflated giant balloon has to be used to lift it to the surface.

The coins and other things which have been brought up are studied by experts.

With the help of old records they try to find out which ship had been carrying the articles, on which date she had sailed and what cargo she was carrying.

If the ship had been carrying valuable cargo, the treasure hunters can go back to the spot and look for it.

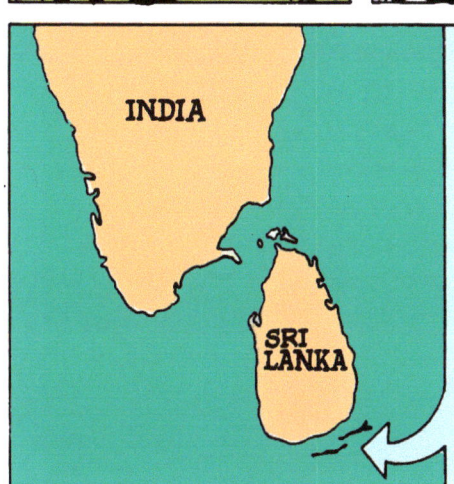

Sunken treasure was found in the Indian Ocean off the southern coast of Sri Lanka on 22nd March 1961 by a team of naturalists. The treasure included Moghul rupees made in Surat in 1702 in the reign of Aurangzeb (1658-1707).

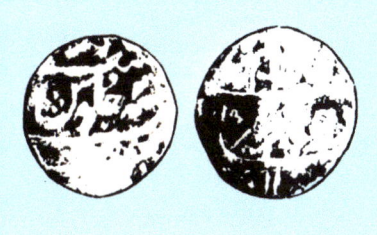

When divers come up too fast!

We breathe air which is a mixture of oxygen and nitrogen gas. When the diver reaches a depth of about 30 metres, he starts breathing in more air than he would do on the surface. The extra nitrogen he takes in gets dissolved in the blood.

Later, when he starts coming up, the nitrogen begins to leave the blood. But if the diver comes up too fast the nitrogen forms bubbles in the blood.

This causes acute pain called 'the bends'.

The only cure is to put the diver into a decompression chamber.

Nitrogen bubbles forming in the lungs

Mooshik
From an idea suggested by V. Shailu, Bangalore

Readers Write...

As I am now in the 8th standard my father keeps saying, "Why do you go on reading comics? The age for reading comics is over." But I can't resist reading TINKLE as there is so much general knowledge in it and so much to learn.

Sailesh Deviah
New Delhi

Both my dog, Lucy and I eagerly wait for TINKLE. I like reading it and Lucy likes biting it!

Dilip Kumar
Bangalore

The other day I was dreaming. Guess what my dream was? I had grown big and was running the TINKLE business along with you! TINKLE had become very popular and each copy cost Rs. 15! After so much profit you and I had grown very rich! My dream would have continued longer if my sister had not woken me up!

Sujoy Gupta
Asansol

See and Smile
Based on an idea suggested by Yogesh Kulkarni, Thane.

Readers' Choice

The Dwarf Who Outwitted the Giant

Illustrations: Ram Waeerkar

Based on a story sent by Praveen Murthy, Bangalore

111

WILL YOU LET ME GO IF YOU CAN'T DO WHAT I DO?
CERTAINLY!
ANYTHING YOU CAN DO, I CAN DO BETTER!
?
NOW LET'S SEE YOU GO THROUGH MY LEGS AS I WENT THROUGH YOURS:
I CAN'T DO IT!
YOU CAN GO! BUT I'LL CATCH YOU AGAIN SOME DAY!
MILIND RAN AWAY AND NEVER WENT THAT WAY AGAIN.

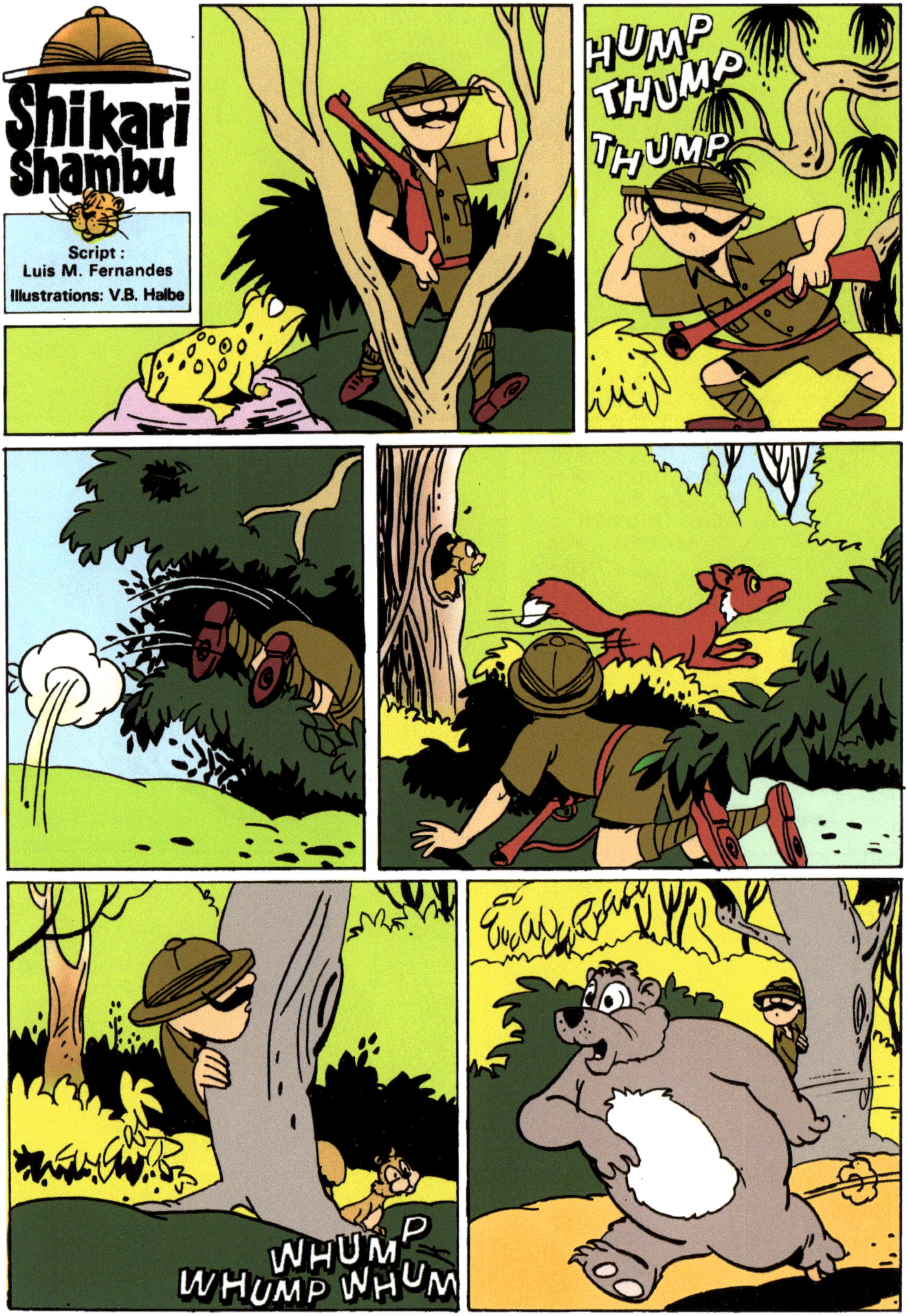

* Refer to the footnote under the Editor's Note

BUMP BUMP BUMP!

FROM WHOM ARE THEY ALL RUNNING AWAY?

ME! THAT MUST BE IT!

THEY'VE HEARD THAT I'M HERE, BUT THEY DON'T KNOW WHERE I AM... HOO HOO!

FEARED AND RESPECTED, THAT'S ME ...HUH!

BEES!

HELP!
SPLASH
SO THAT'S WHAT THEY WERE ALL RUNNING AWAY FROM!
ANYWAY, I'M SAFE HERE.
EH!
!

SUNDAR AND THE SETH

Based on a story sent by Avlok, New Delhi

Illustrations: V. B. Halbe

"HEY, SONU! NO WORK TODAY?"

"I'VE STOPPED WORKING FOR SETHJI."

"I'D RATHER STARVE THAN WORK FOR HIM."

"WHY? WHAT HAPPENED?"

"HE DID NOT PAY ME A PAISA AND... HE WAS ABOUT TO... C...CUT OFF MY NOSE."

"HOW AWFUL! BUT, WHY?"

"BECAUSE THAT WAS HIS CONDITION WHEN HE HIRED ME. IF I LEFT HIS SERVICE, HE COULD CUT OFF MY NOSE AND IF HE SACKED ME, I COULD CUT OFF HIS NOSE."

"HOW STRANGE!"

"YOUR SETHJI SOUNDS LIKE AN INTERESTING MAN."

"I'LL GO AND OFFER MY SERVICES TO HIM."

!

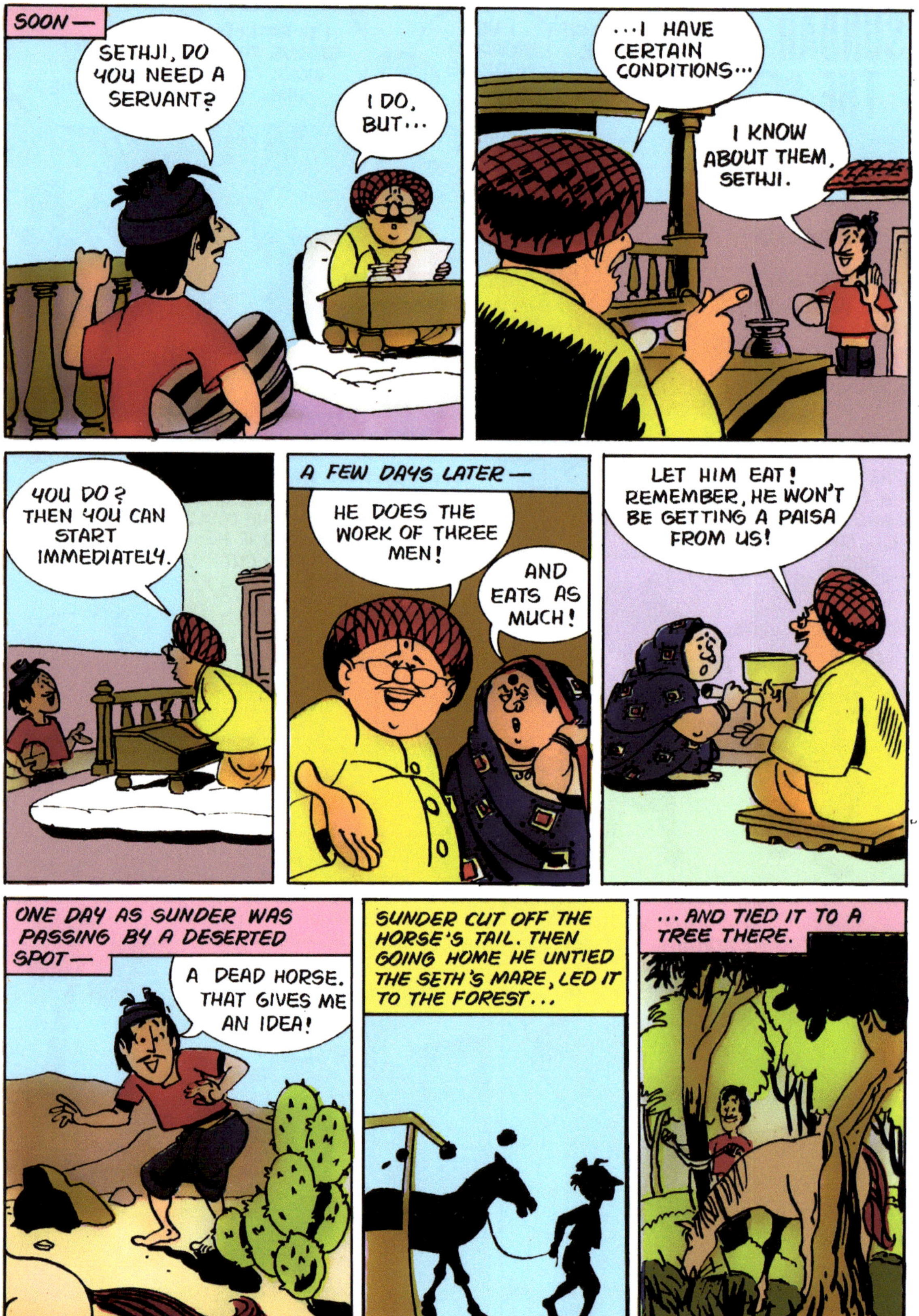
SOON—
SETHJI, DO YOU NEED A SERVANT?
I DO, BUT...
...I HAVE CERTAIN CONDITIONS...
I KNOW ABOUT THEM, SETHJI.
YOU DO? THEN YOU CAN START IMMEDIATELY.
A FEW DAYS LATER—
HE DOES THE WORK OF THREE MEN!
AND EATS AS MUCH!
LET HIM EAT! REMEMBER, HE WON'T BE GETTING A PAISA FROM US!
ONE DAY AS SUNDER WAS PASSING BY A DESERTED SPOT—
A DEAD HORSE. THAT GIVES ME AN IDEA!
SUNDER CUT OFF THE HORSE'S TAIL. THEN GOING HOME HE UNTIED THE SETH'S MARE, LED IT TO THE FOREST...
...AND TIED IT TO A TREE THERE.

AFTERWARDS HE PLANTED THE HORSE'S TAIL IN A MARSHY SPOT...
...AND RAN HOME.
SETHJI! SETHJI! YOUR MARE IS SINKING IN THE MARSH. HURRY! HURRY!
OH!
LOOK! IT'S GONE IN!
OH, THE POOR MARE!
SPLOSH
!
SETHJI, YOU HAVE KILLED YOUR MARE. NOW YOU'LL HAVE TO GIVE A FEAST TO ATONE FOR YOUR SIN.
A... FEAST?

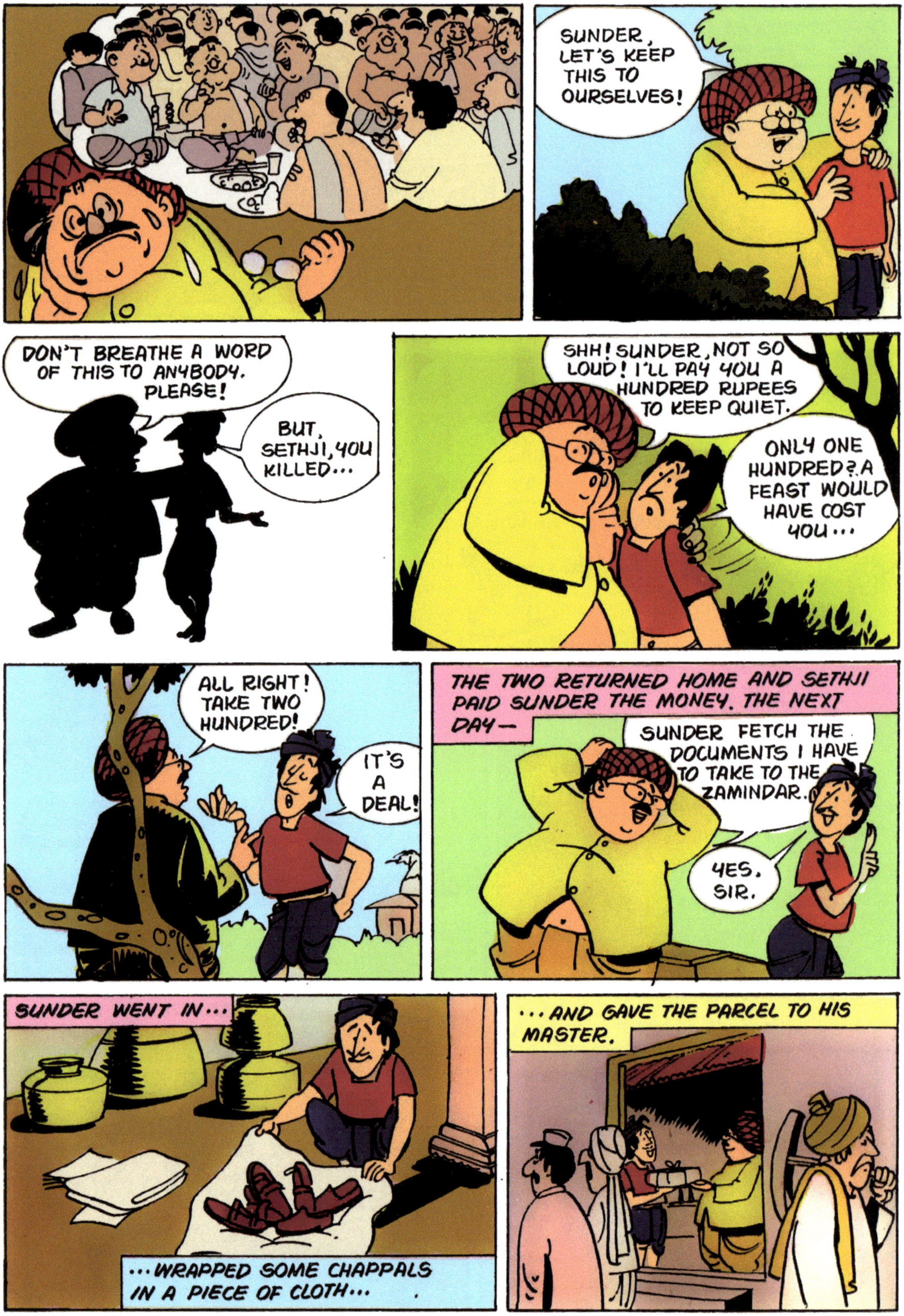

SUNDER, LET'S KEEP THIS TO OURSELVES!
DON'T BREATHE A WORD OF THIS TO ANYBODY. PLEASE!
BUT, SETHJI, YOU KILLED...
SHH! SUNDER, NOT SO LOUD! I'LL PAY YOU A HUNDRED RUPEES TO KEEP QUIET.
ONLY ONE HUNDRED? A FEAST WOULD HAVE COST YOU...
ALL RIGHT! TAKE TWO HUNDRED!
IT'S A DEAL!
THE TWO RETURNED HOME AND SETHJI PAID SUNDER THE MONEY. THE NEXT DAY—
SUNDER FETCH THE DOCUMENTS I HAVE TO TAKE TO THE ZAMINDAR.
YES. SIR.
SUNDER WENT IN...
...WRAPPED SOME CHAPPALS IN A PIECE OF CLOTH...
...AND GAVE THE PARCEL TO HIS MASTER.

AT THE ZAMINDAR'S HOUSE—
I HAVE BROUGHT THE PAPERS, SIR.
HERE THEY... OH! OH!
HA! HA! HA!
THE SETH RETURNED HOME, FUMING WITH RAGE—
YOU... YOU...!
YES, SETHJI?
YOU ROGUE! HOW DARE YOU INSULT ME!
I DIDN'T DO A THING SETHJI...
...YET YOU CAN SACK ME IF YOU LIKE!
I WILL!
YOU'RE... YOU'RE...! NEVER MIND!
A FEW DAYS LATER, WHEN SETHJI HAD TO GO TO HIS FATHER-IN-LAW'S HOUSE...
...SUNDER FOLLOWED HIM QUIETLY...

...AND TAKING A SHORTER ROUTE, REACHED AHEAD OF HIS MASTER.
NAMASKAR, SIR! I AM A SERVANT OF YOUR SON-IN-LAW SETHJI IS ON HIS WAY HERE.
SETHANI HAS SENT ME TO TELL YOU THAT ONLY GREEN CHILLIES AND BLACK SALT SHOULD BE GIVEN TO HIM AS FOOD.
GREEN CHILLIES AND SALT?
A SPECIAL DIET, SIR. HE IS NOT WELL, YOU KNOW.
WHAT IS WRONG WITH HIM?
HE IS... SUFFERING... FROM BRAIN-FEVER... BEHAVES STRANGELY AT TIMES.
OH, MY GOD!
SETHJI ARRIVED A LITTLE LATER. AT LUNCH TIME —
HERE IS YOUR SPECIAL LUNCH, SON-IN-LAW.
SPECIAL LUNCH... THIS?
YES, YOUR SERVANT HAS TOLD US ALL.
MY SERVANT?

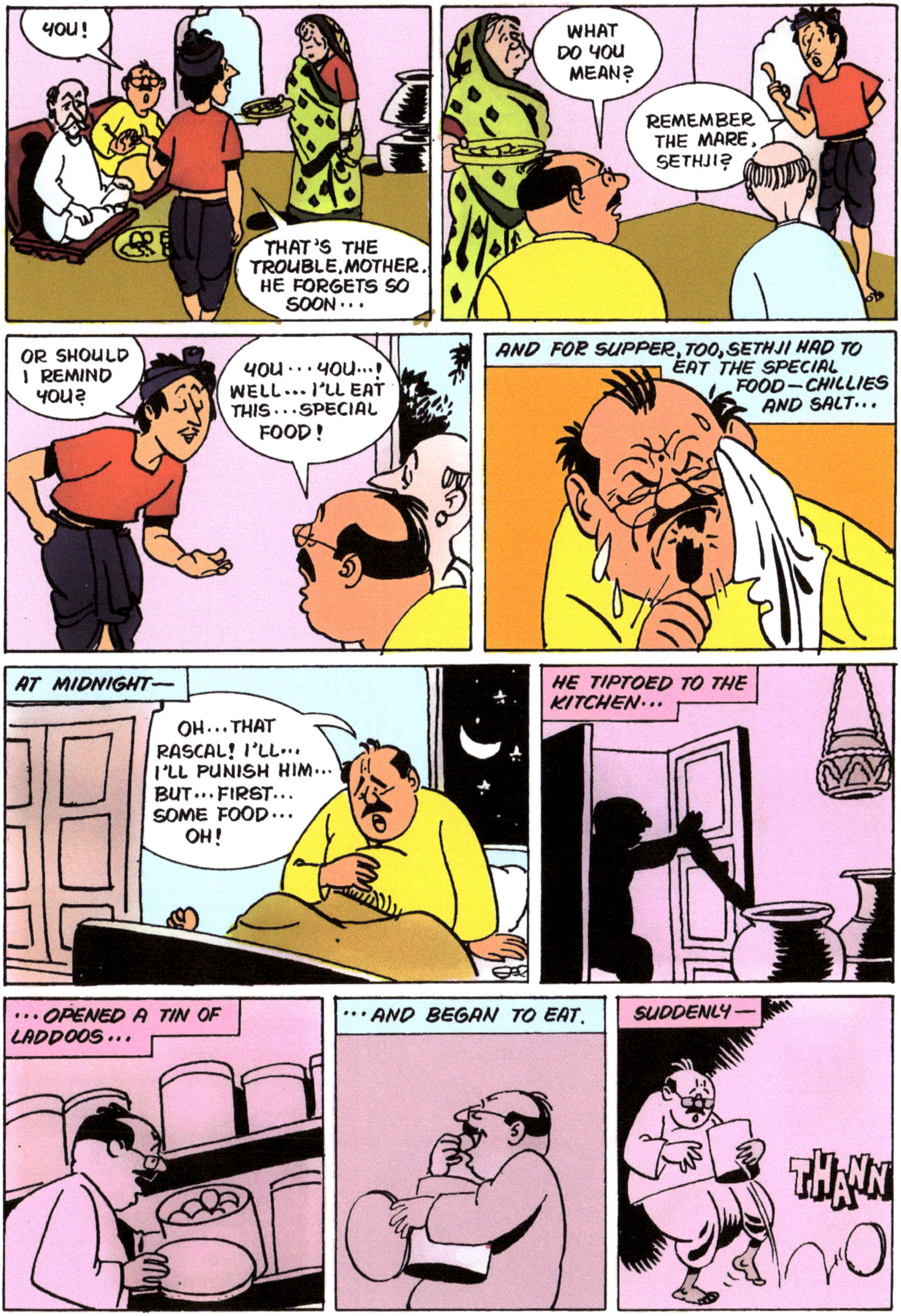
YOU!
THAT'S THE TROUBLE, MOTHER. HE FORGETS SO SOON...
WHAT DO YOU MEAN?
REMEMBER THE MARE, SETHJI?
OR SHOULD I REMIND YOU?
YOU... YOU...! WELL... I'LL EAT THIS... SPECIAL FOOD!
AND FOR SUPPER, TOO, SETHJI HAD TO EAT THE SPECIAL FOOD—CHILLIES AND SALT...
AT MIDNIGHT—
OH... THAT RASCAL! I'LL... I'LL PUNISH HIM... BUT... FIRST... SOME FOOD... OH!
HE TIPTOED TO THE KITCHEN...
...OPENED A TIN OF LADDOOS...
...AND BEGAN TO EAT.
SUDDENLY—
THANN

WHO...WHO IS THERE!!

IT'S A THIEF! HELP! HELP!

GET A LIGHT SOMEONE!

I AM COMING!

WHAT! YOU!

I....I....

...I'LL EXPLAIN! BUT PLEASE LET ME EAT FIRST. I AM FAMISHED!

THE NEXT MORNING SETHJI CALLED SUNDER ASIDE...

SUNDER! CUT OFF MY NOSE! DO ANYTHING BUT...

...PLEASE LEAVE ME! I BEG YOU! I HAVE HAD ENOUGH.

BUT SUNDER DID NOT CUT OFF THE SETH'S NOSE. HE ACCEPTED FIVE HUNDRED RUPEES AND RETURNED HOME. HE GAVE THE SETH'S MARE TO HIS FRIEND, SONU.

Readers' Choice

THE KING OF BIRDS

Illustrations: Ashok Dongre

Based on a story sent by Anil Madan, New Delhi

ONE DAY ALL THE BIRDS IN THE FOREST MET TO CHOOSE A KING.

"THE PEACOCK SHOULD BE KING."

"I CAN BE A KING TOO!"

"WHY NOT ME?"

"THE KING OF BIRDS MUST BE THE ONE WHO CAN FLY HIGHER THAN THE REST...."

"I AGREE WITH SIR EAGLE."

"SO DO I."

"I DON'T."

"LET'S ALL SIT ON THIS BRANCH. WHEN THE DUCK QUACKS, WE'LL FLY UP INTO THE SKY... AND THE ONE WHO FLIES HIGHEST WILL BE MADE KING."

MOVE OVER.
DON'T PUSH!
A LITTLE LATER—
READY? STEADY? QUACK! QUACK!
MY WINGS ARE ACHING. I CAN'T FLY ANY HIGHER.
ONE BY ONE, ALL THE BIRDS DROPPED OUT OF THE RACE...
AND FINALLY ONLY THE EAGLE WAS LEFT—
I CAN'T FLY ANY MORE... BUT IT DOESN'T MATTER.

I HAVE WON...
EH!
THE WREN! IT WAS RIDING ON MY BACK!
AS THE TIRED EAGLE FELL BACK TO THE EARTH—
THE WREN SOARED HIGH INTO THE AIR...
... AND WON THE CONTEST.
THE WREN IS OUR KING.
HURRAH!
ASHOK DONGRE

MEET THE MULE

Script: Ashvin
Illustrations: Pradeep Sathe

WHO ARE THE PARENTS OF THIS BUFFALO-CALF?

ITS MOTHER IS A SHE-BUFFALO AND ITS FATHER IS A HE-BUFFALO.

NOW, WHO ARE THE PARENTS OF THIS BABY MULE?

IF YOU SAY A SHE-MULE AND A HE-MULE, YOU WOULD BE TOTALLY WRONG.

BECAUSE ITS MOTHER IS A MARE (FEMALE HORSE) AND ITS FATHER IS A JACK (MALE DONKEY).

THE HORSE AND THE DONKEY ARE CLOSE RELATIVES AND CAN MATE, IF THEY DON'T FIND A MATE OF THEIR OWN SPECIES.

THE ANIMAL PRODUCED BY THE ANIMALS OF TWO DIFFERENT SPECIES IS CALLED A CROSSBREED OR HYBRID.

LOOK AT THIS ADULT MULE! IT IS AS LARGE AS ITS MOTHER AND ITS TAIL IS LIKE HERS.

BUT IT HAS GOT LONG EARS AND SMALL HOOFS FROM ITS FATHER.

MULES ARE MORE INTELLIGENT THAN EITHER OF THEIR PARENTS. SOME KINGS IN THE PAST RODE MULES IN PREFERENCE TO HORSES.

THE MULE CAN CARRY HEAVY LOADS. BECAUSE OF ITS LARGE SIZE IT CAN CARRY MORE LOAD (ALMOST DOUBLE) THAN THE DONKEY.

IT'S NOT FUSSY ABOUT FOOD EITHER...

...IT CAN FEED ON BRUSH.

THE MULE CAN WALK FAIRLY FAST TOO, AND IT IS SURE-FOOTED.

BUT IT IS SOMEWHAT STUBBORN AND ILL-TEMPERED. NO ONE CAN MAKE IT WORK IF IT DOESN'T WANT TO.

AND A KICK OF ITS HIND LEGS IS VERY DANGEROUS. DURING WORLD WAR I, MULES WERE USED TO PULL HEAVY CANNON GUNS AND CARTS. AT THAT TIME, MULES BROKE MANY A SOLDIER'S JAW.

IN MODERN TIMES WHEN MAN HAS MACHINES LIKE HELICOPTERS TO TRANSPORT GOODS, MULES ARE NOT USED AS MUCH AS THEY ONCE WERE.

MULES ARE STERILE — THAT IS, THEY CAN'T HAVE OFFSPRING. SO THERE IS NO WAY OF REPRODUCING THEM EXCEPT THROUGH CROSSBREEDING.

* Refer to the footnote under the Editor's Note

EDITOR'S CHOICE

My young friends,

Once upon a time a group of onions lived together in a village. The onions lived a lonely life as they had no friends.

One day an old onion thought to himself: "When we die no one will cry for us."

So the old onion went to the jungle and began to meditate. After a long time, Lord Brahma appeared before him. He was pleased with the onion.

"What is it that you need?" asked Brahma.

"Lord ... Lord ...," the onion replied.

"Do not hesitate. Speak," said Brahma.

The onion gathered courage and said, "Lord, we have no friends. When we die there will be no one to weep for us."

Brahma was moved. "Don't worry. I will solve your problem. From now on, whenever any one cuts you, he himself will cry for you."

"Thank you, Lord," said the onion, overjoyed.

Brahma disappeared and the happy onion went back to his village.

Thus, whenever we cut onions, tears roll down our eyes!

Master Ganesh Iyer of Valsad sent me this story.

Affectionately yours,

Uncle Pai

Ganesh Iyer

Tinkle Tricks & Treats* TTT-35

A What's unusual here?

B One of these is not an Asian flag. Which one?

1.
2.
3.
4.

C Put these pictures in order.

A B C

* Refer to the footnote under the Editor's Note

SOLUTIONS OF TTT NO. 35

A—No. 4. The Canadian flag

B—The boy's shirt has one long sleeve and one short sleeve.

C—B, C, A.

Make an Ice Cream Stick Puppet

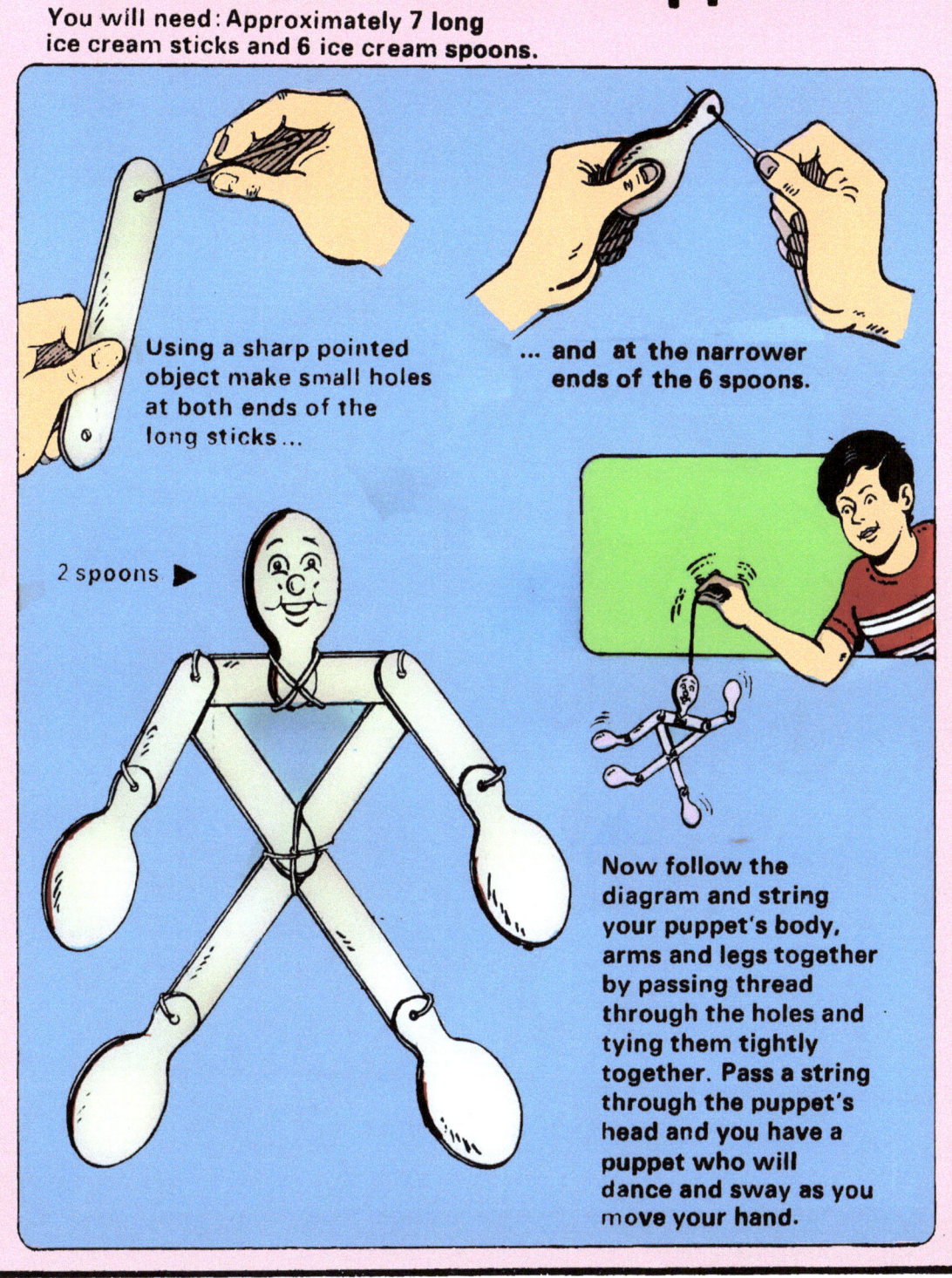

You will need: Approximately 7 long ice cream sticks and 6 ice cream spoons.

Using a sharp pointed object make small holes at both ends of the long sticks...

...and at the narrower ends of the 6 spoons.

◀ 2 spoons

Now follow the diagram and string your puppet's body, arms and legs together by passing thread through the holes and tying them tightly together. Pass a string through the puppet's head and you have a puppet who will dance and sway as you move your hand.

NO. 44   Rs. 3

TINKLE

THE FORTNIGHTLY FOR CHILDREN FROM THE HOUSE OF AMAR CHITRA KATHA

THE KING OF BIRDS

MEET THE MULE

GRANDMA GOES VISITING

ABOUT ANWAR

If you love the wisecracks of Anwar ever since he made his debut in *Tinkle* 39 (1983), then you have Mr. Subba Rao to thank. Mr. Rao, one of the founding editors of *Tinkle*, is the writer behind Anwar's varied shenanigans. When asked how he came up with such a loveable rogue, he quips, "My son, Siddharth, gets all the credit for the creation of Anwar. He was around three or four years old at the time when I started the strip, and his antics and naïve observations inspired all the Anwar comics."

Here is a glimpse into one of Siddharth's charmingly naïve observations that reflects in Anwar's persona. Mr. Rao and the then *Tinkle* editorial team's story creation process was collaborative. The team had storytelling sessions wherein each member would share stories. They were all so enthusiastic that working for *Tinkle* became an absolute delight. One day, Siddharth visited the office and witnessed the team in action. When he went back home, he complained to his mother, "Appa is just having a lot of fun in the office. He isn't working at all!"

Siddharth inspired more than Anwar, though; he also partly inspired Mr. Rao's pseudonym Appaswami. In fact, Mr. Rao published all his Anwar stories under this name. Siddharth called his father 'Appa', while Mr. Rao's wife called him 'Swami', a respectful term for one's husband. Mr. Rao simply put those two names together, and hey presto! Appaswami was born.

Just as Mr. Rao keenly observed his son for ideas, he also watched other children's behaviour. He says, "I'm as curious as a child about everything that happens around me… Also, I like spending time with children. Their mischief is very inspiring." Just like children's mischief, Anwar's witticisms too are evergreen and they still give readers a good chuckle.

Nasruddin Hodja

WHY ARE YOU SITTING THERE, HODJA?

SOONER OR LATER SOMETHING WILL HAPPEN HERE AND A CROWD WILL GATHER.

THEN I MAY NOT BE ABLE TO GET CLOSE ENOUGH TO SEE WHAT'S HAPPENING...

...SO I AM RESERVING MY SEAT NOW!

Readers Write...

I spent my holidays in Bhopal. My grandmother was in hospital with a broken foot. Every day from the house to the hospital and back, we used to pass Akashwani. One day I noticed a radio telescope behind the building. So I showed it to my mother who asked me how I knew it was a radio telescope. I told her that I knew about it because it was behind the Akashwani and it looked very much like the one I had read about in TINKLE. My mother was pleased that I read things on science and not only stories in TINKLE.

Vikramaditya Ugra
Bombay

The labels which you gave us in TINKLE No. 36 were liked by all. When our teacher saw my notebooks, she recognised them immediately. "Oh, so you read TINKLE! Keep it up – it's a very good habit," she said. Next time, please give us more of them because you gave us only eight and our books are more than two dozen!

Beheroze Sattha
Bombay

Recently there was a quiz competition on animals in my school. I answered all the questions and got first prize, all because of TINKLE!

Gowhar Ali
Kashmir

Mooshik

Based on an idea suggested by K.L. Sunitha, Bangalore

Mooshik
From an idea suggested by Jairaj P., Calicut

To Our Readers*

TINKLE SUBSCRIPTIONS:
All new subscriptions and renewals of the old ones are accepted at:

PARTHA BOOKS DIVISION
Nav Prabhat Chambers, Ranade Road, Dadar, Bombay 400 028.
The annual subscription rate for 24 issues is Rs. 72/- per year (add Rs. 3/- on outstation cheques). Drafts/cheques/M.O. should be in favour of PARTHA BOOKS DIVISION.

Readers' Contributions should be addressed to Editor, TINKLE, Mahalaxmi Chambers (Basement), 22 Bhulabhai Desai Road, Bombay 400 026.

Mooshik:
Rs. 10/- will be paid for every original idea accepted.

Readers' Choice:
* Please send only folktales you have heard and not those you have read in books, magazines or textbooks. Rs. 25/- will be paid for every accepted contribution.
* Send a self-addressed stamped envelope if you want the story to be returned.
* Please do not send photographs until asked for.

This happened to me:
You can write on your own strange, thrilling or amusing experience or adventure. Rs. 15/- will be paid for every accepted contribution.

Readers Write...
1. Mail your letters to: Tinkle. P. Bag No. 16541, Bombay 400 026.
2. Please give your address in your letters, if you want a reply.

TINKLE TRICKS AND TREATS

1. Mail your entry to: Tinkle Competition Section, P. Bag No. 16541, Bombay 400 026.
2. The first 50 all-correct entries received by us will each win a set of personal letterheads, with the winners names and addresses printed on them!
3. The next 350 all-correct entries received by us will each win a copy of the AMAR INDIA WALL PAPER No. 19 dated November 1983

* Refer to the footnote under the Editor's Note

------ CUT HERE

ENTRY FORM*   **MY SOLUTIONS**   TTT-35

NAME: _____

ADDRESS: _____

STATE: _____

A _____

B _____

C _____

Readers' Choice

THE CAT AND THE TIGER

Illustrations: Pradeep Sathe

Based on a story sent by D.N. Venkatachalam, Bangalore

Panel 1:
Tiger: "YOU'VE BEEN A REMARKABLE TEACHER, BUT YOU HAVEN'T SHOWN ME HOW TO CLIMB A TREE."
Cat (thinking): "AHA! SO THAT'S IT!"

Panel 2:
Cat: "COME, I'LL SHOW YOU HOW."
Tiger (thinking): "AT LAST!"

Panel 3:
Tiger (thinking): "!?"

Panel 4:
Tiger: "BROTHER CAT! COME DOWN! I HAVEN'T LEARNT IT YET."
Cat: "BROTHER TIGER, IF I TEACH YOU HOW TO CLIMB TREES, I'LL NEVER BE SAFE FROM YOU...."

Panel 5:
Cat: "SO GO HOME — THIS IS ONE THING YOU'LL NEVER LEARN!"

AND TIGERS STILL DON'T KNOW HOW TO CLIMB TREES.

GRANDMA GOES VISITING

Illustrations: M. Mohandas

Based on a story sent by Vijay Kewalramani, New Kandla

Readers' Choice

AND SO—
AFTER A WHILE—
THE LION!
WELL, WELL! HERE COMES MY LUNCH.
WHERE ARE YOU GOING OLD WOMAN?
T-TO MY SON'S HOUSE. TO SEE MY G-GRANDSON.
I'LL GO WITH HER AND EAT THEM ALL.
TAKE ME WITH YOU.
A-ALL RIGHT.
SOON—
HEY! THAT'S GRANDMA! ON A POT! AND···
···AND THE WICKED LION!

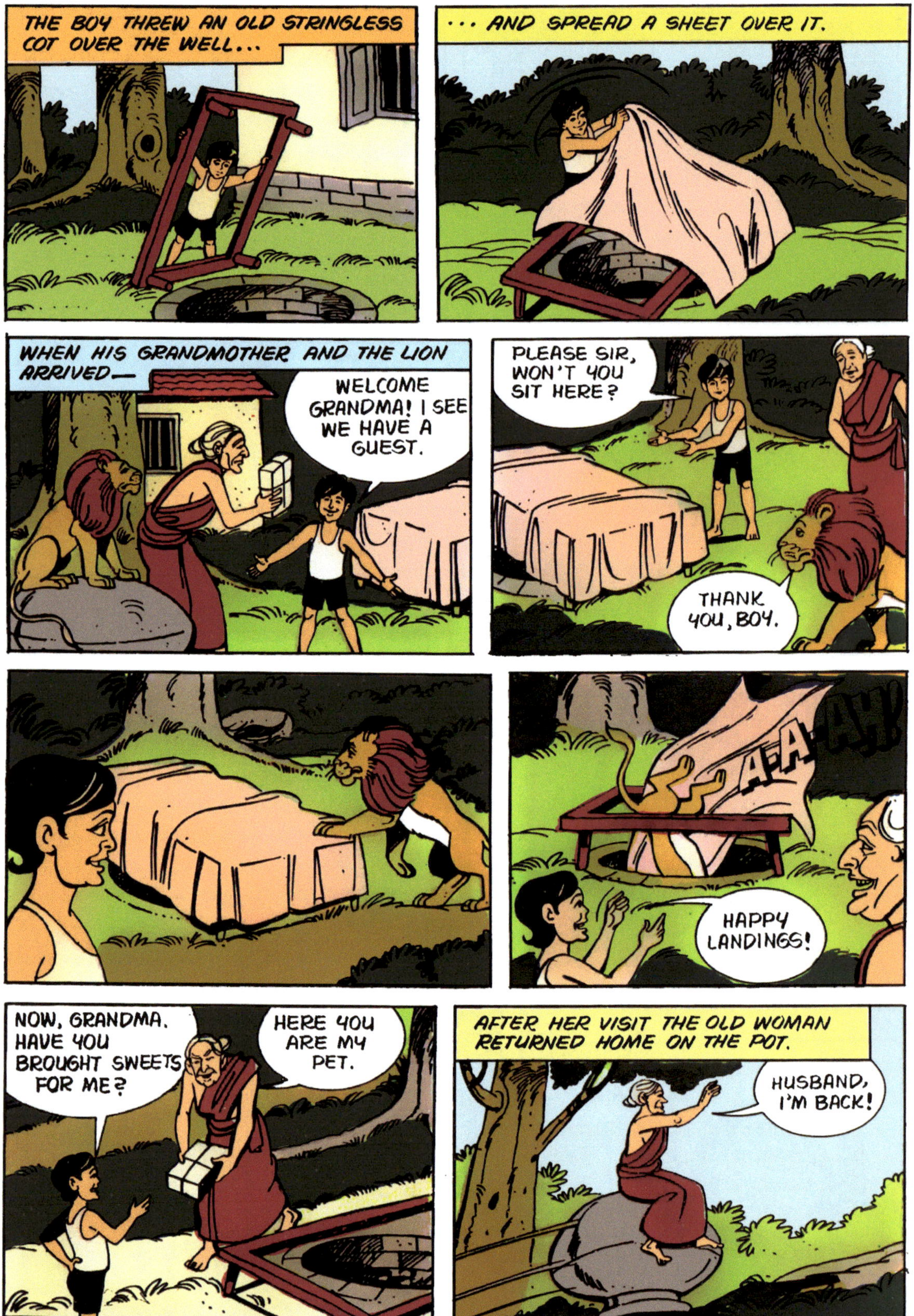
THE BOY THREW AN OLD STRINGLESS COT OVER THE WELL...
... AND SPREAD A SHEET OVER IT.
WHEN HIS GRANDMOTHER AND THE LION ARRIVED—
WELCOME GRANDMA! I SEE WE HAVE A GUEST.
PLEASE SIR, WON'T YOU SIT HERE?
THANK YOU, BOY.
A-A-AH!
HAPPY LANDINGS!
NOW, GRANDMA. HAVE YOU BROUGHT SWEETS FOR ME?
HERE YOU ARE MY PET.
AFTER HER VISIT THE OLD WOMAN RETURNED HOME ON THE POT.
HUSBAND, I'M BACK!

The race to the moon

Script: J.D. Isloor **Illustrations:** Anand Mande

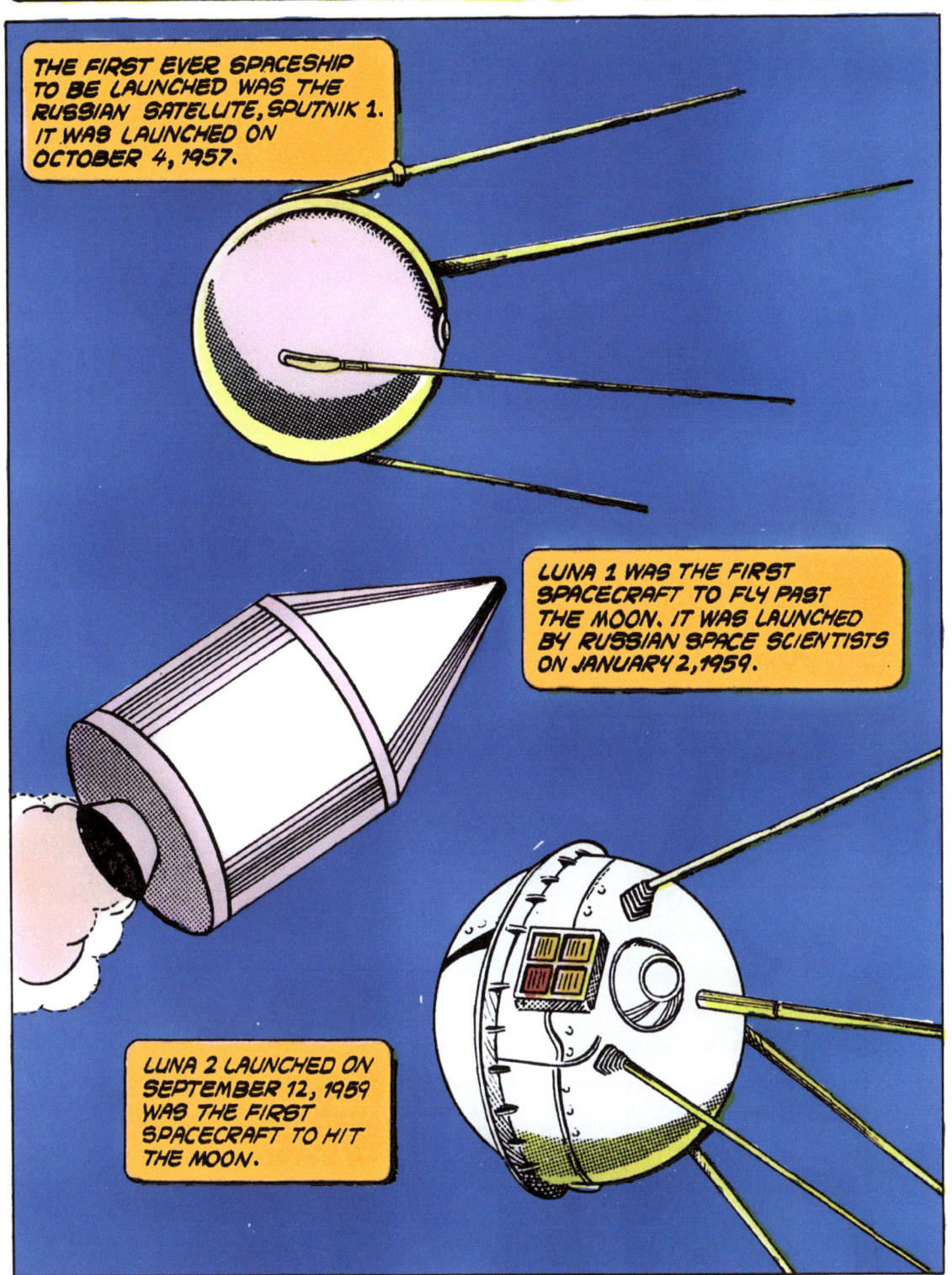

THE FIRST EVER SPACESHIP TO BE LAUNCHED WAS THE RUSSIAN SATELLITE, SPUTNIK 1. IT WAS LAUNCHED ON OCTOBER 4, 1957.

LUNA 1 WAS THE FIRST SPACECRAFT TO FLY PAST THE MOON. IT WAS LAUNCHED BY RUSSIAN SPACE SCIENTISTS ON JANUARY 2, 1959.

LUNA 2 LAUNCHED ON SEPTEMBER 12, 1959 WAS THE FIRST SPACECRAFT TO HIT THE MOON.

LUNA 3 WAS LAUNCHED ON OCTOBER 4, 1959. THIS SPACECRAFT TOOK PHOTOGRAPHS OF THE FAR SIDE OF THE MOON WHICH HAD NEVER BEEN SEEN BEFORE. THIS IS BECAUSE THE MOON ALWAYS HAS THE SAME SIDE TURNED TOWARDS THE EARTH.

AMERICAN ATTEMPTS TO REACH THE MOON WERE NOT SUCCESSFUL UNTIL JULY 1964 WHEN A RANGER 7 SPACECRAFT SENT BACK PICTURES BEFORE IT CRASHED ON THE MOON.

BOTH RUSSIAN AND AMERICAN SCIENTISTS BEGAN TO DESIGN SPACECRAFTS THAT WOULD NOT CRASH, BUT LAND GENTLY ON THE MOON. IN 1966 THE RUSSIANS SUCCEEDED IN LANDING A SPACECRAFT GENTLY ON THE MOON. THIS SPACECRAFT, LUNA 9, SENT BACK THE FIRST CLOSE-UP PICTURES OF THE MOON'S SURFACE.

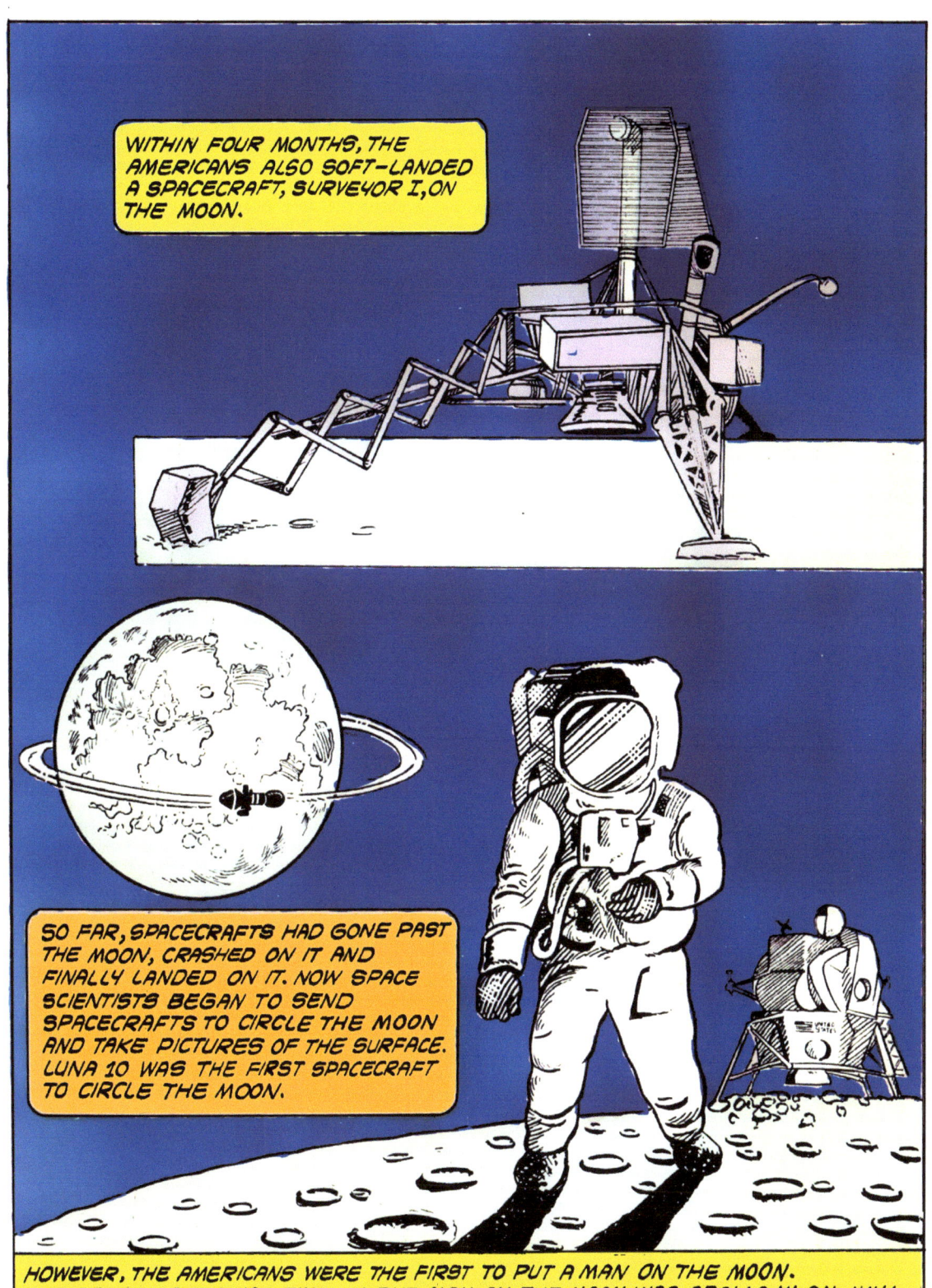

WITHIN FOUR MONTHS, THE AMERICANS ALSO SOFT-LANDED A SPACECRAFT, SURVEYOR I, ON THE MOON.

SO FAR, SPACECRAFTS HAD GONE PAST THE MOON, CRASHED ON IT AND FINALLY LANDED ON IT. NOW SPACE SCIENTISTS BEGAN TO SEND SPACECRAFTS TO CIRCLE THE MOON AND TAKE PICTURES OF THE SURFACE. LUNA 10 WAS THE FIRST SPACECRAFT TO CIRCLE THE MOON.

HOWEVER, THE AMERICANS WERE THE FIRST TO PUT A MAN ON THE MOON. THE SPACECRAFT THAT FINALLY PUT MAN ON THE MOON WAS APOLLO XI ON JULY 21, 1969. AS NEIL ARMSTRONG STEPPED ON THE MOON'S SURFACE, HIS FIRST WORDS WERE: "THAT'S ONE SMALL STEP FOR MAN, ONE GIANT LEAP FOR MANKIND."

Kalia
THE CROW
Script:
LUIS
Illustrations:
PRADEEP SATHE
I NEVER CATCH ANY PREY WHEN THIS IDIOT IS WITH ME.
ER... DOOB DOOB, LET'S SEPARATE.
EH!
I'LL GO AFTER THAT RABBIT AND YOU GO AFTER THAT DEER.
I DON'T THINK I COULD CATCH A DEER, CHAMATAKA. THEY'RE TOO FAST.
HEY, I KNOW HOW YOU CAN GET CLOSE TO THAT DEER...
LISTEN...
SOON—
HEY, SHONAR!
DOOB! DOOB!
DON'T RUN AWAY! WAIT! YOUR FRIEND KALIA IS IN TROUBLE!

WHAT?!
ALL HIS FEATHERS SUDDENLY FELL OFF. SEE, THIS IS ONE OF HIS FEATHERS.
OH, MY POOR FRIEND!
I'M CLOSE ENOUGH NOW, I'LL LASH OUT WITH MY TAIL AND...
IS SOMEONE IN TROUBLE?
HE SAYS KALIA HAS LOST ALL HIS FEATHERS.
WHAT?!
I... I...
WHAT'S THE MATTER?
KALIA IS IN TROUBLE.
?
HE HAS LOST ALL HIS FEATHERS.
WHERE'S HE? PLEASE TAKE US TO HIM.
I...UH...ALL RIGHT.
CHAMATAKA AND HIS STUPID IDEAS! NOW WHERE CAN I TAKE ALL THESE ANIMALS? AND WHAT IF WE SHOULD MEET KALIA ON THE WAY!

I'LL TAKE YOU TO WHERE I SAW HIM LAST. BUT HE MUST'VE FLOWN AWAY BY NOW.
HOW CAN HE FLY AWAY IF HE HAS LOST ALL HIS FEATHERS?
Y-YOU'RE RIGHT.
MEANWHILE, NOT FAR AWAY —
GOT YOU!
LET ME GO! LET ME GO!
NOT A CHANCE!
?!
WHERE IS DOOB DOOB TAKING THOSE ANIMALS?
I'D BETTER HIDE TILL THEY'VE GONE PAST.

HOW MUCH FURTHER?
ER... HE IS IN THAT BUSH OVER THERE.
THERE IS NO ONE HERE...
YES THERE IS...
...CHAMATAKA!
I...ER...I...UH WAS TALKING TO THIS LITTLE RABBIT.
GO AWAY LITTLE RABBIT... DID YOU THINK I WOULD EAT YOU? HA HA HA...
WHAT HAVE YOU DONE WITH KALIA!
KALIA?
HOW WAS I TO KNOW HE WAS HIDING THERE...I'D BETTER GET OUT OF HERE.
WHAT'S GOING ON THERE, DOOB DOOB?
CHAMATAKA HAS GOT HIMSELF INTO SOME TROUBLE!

Echo and Narcissus

A tale from Greek Mythology

Script: Anand Kumar Raju
Illustrations: Pradeep Sathe

ECHO, THE NYMPH, WAS VERY TALKATIVE—

"AND THEN I SAW THE DEER RUNNING AWAY. I FOLLOWED IT...."

"ECHO, PLEASE STOP. YOU'VE BEEN TALKING FOR HOURS. I'M TIRED."

"BUT LISTEN, I HAVEN'T TOLD YOU WHAT HAPPENED AFTER THAT."

"ECHO, PLEASE, ENOUGH. I'M GOING."

"SHE'S GONE!"

JUST THEN, THE MOTHER OF THE GODS, HERA, CAME THAT WAY.

"ECHO, HAVE YOU SEEN MY HUSBAND, ZEUS?"

"NO, MOTHER HERA, I HAVEN'T SEEN FATHER ZEUS."

"BUT I'M SURE I SAW HIM COME HERE."

"HE HASN'T BEEN HERE, MOTHER HERA!"

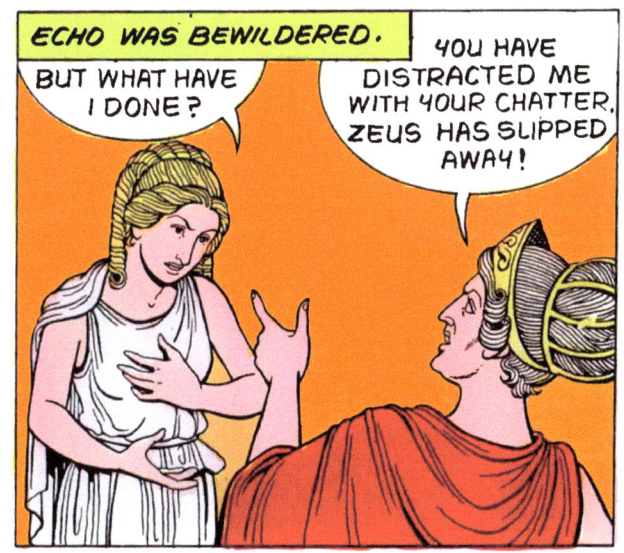

Panel 1:
"BUT I HEARD VOICES!"
"I WAS TELLING MY FRIEND WHAT HAPPENED THIS MORNING."

Panel 2:
"WHAT HAPPENED?"
"I SAW A DEER RUNNING NEAR THE RIVER AND..."

ECHO TALKED AND TALKED...

Panel 3:
...UNTIL—
"OH DO BE QUIET! SEE WHAT YOU HAVE DONE!"

Panel 4:
ECHO WAS BEWILDERED.
"BUT WHAT HAVE I DONE?"
"YOU HAVE DISTRACTED ME WITH YOUR CHATTER. ZEUS HAS SLIPPED AWAY!"

Panel 5:
"YOU SILLY GIRL! FROM NOW ON, YOU'LL NEVER BE ABLE TO TALK. YOU WILL ONLY REPEAT THE LAST WORD OF WHATEVER ANYONE SAYS."
"...ANYONE SAYS!"

Panel 6:
POOR ECHO COULD NO LONGER SPEAK AND WANDERED ABOUT BY HERSELF.

ONE DAY A HANDSOME LAD CALLED NARCISSUS CAME TO THE FOREST. AND SHE FELL IN LOVE WITH HIM.
AS SHE FOLLOWED HIM AROUND—
WHO ARE YOU, GIRL?
...GIRL.
I KNOW THAT YOU ARE A GIRL. WHAT IS YOUR NAME?
...NAME.
OH, GO AWAY YOU SILLY GIRL. YOU ARE STUPID.
...STUPID.
HOW DARE YOU CALL ME STUPID, YOU WRETCHED CREATURE!
...CREA-TURE.
NARCISSUS WENT AWAY IN ANGER LEAVING ECHO ALONE.
ECHO, HEART-BROKEN, MELTED INTO A SPIRIT, WATCHED BY NEMESIS, THE GODDESS OF REVENGE.

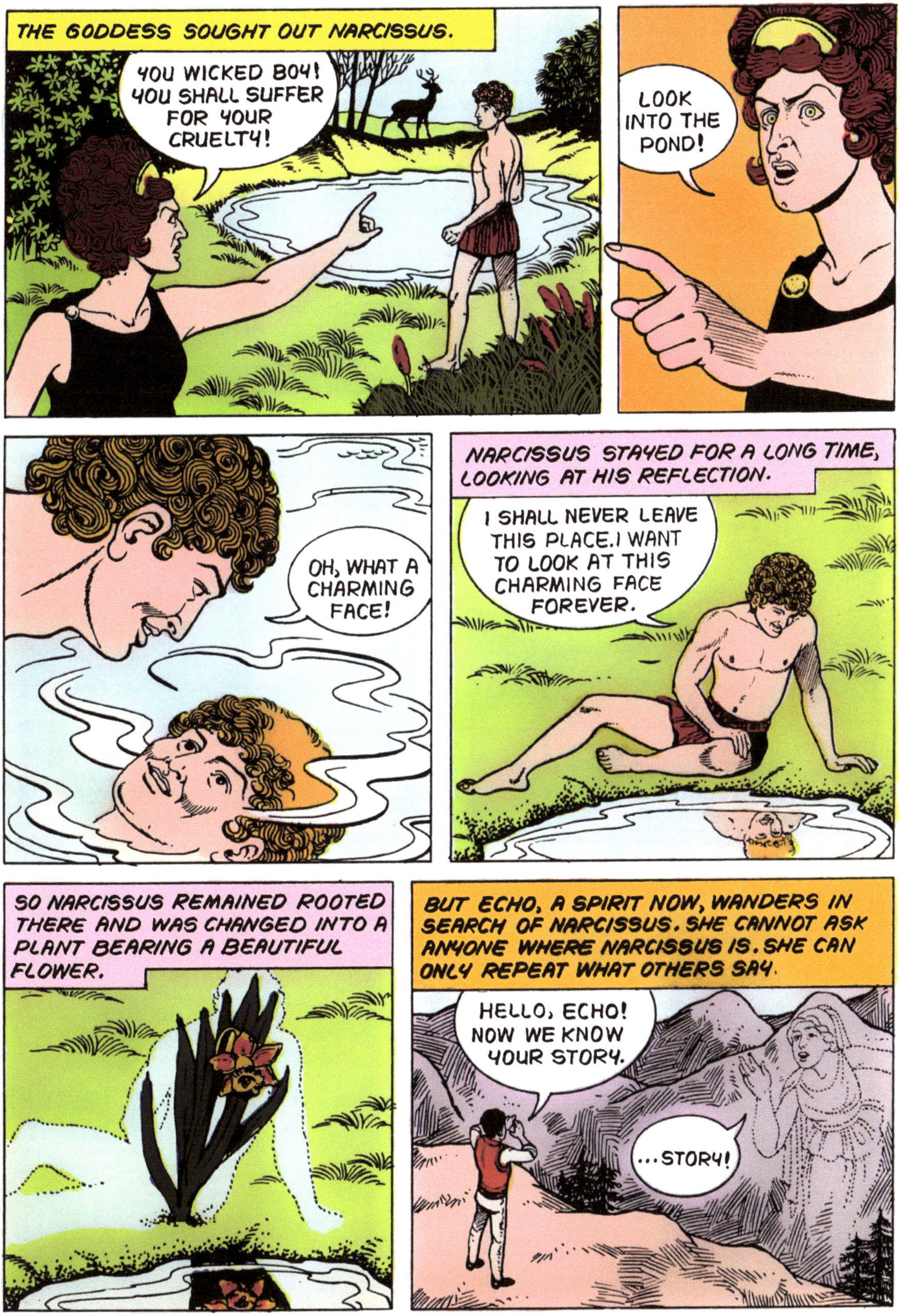
THE GODDESS SOUGHT OUT NARCISSUS.
YOU WICKED BOY! YOU SHALL SUFFER FOR YOUR CRUELTY!
LOOK INTO THE POND!
OH, WHAT A CHARMING FACE!
NARCISSUS STAYED FOR A LONG TIME, LOOKING AT HIS REFLECTION.
I SHALL NEVER LEAVE THIS PLACE. I WANT TO LOOK AT THIS CHARMING FACE FOREVER.
SO NARCISSUS REMAINED ROOTED THERE AND WAS CHANGED INTO A PLANT BEARING A BEAUTIFUL FLOWER.
BUT ECHO, A SPIRIT NOW, WANDERS IN SEARCH OF NARCISSUS. SHE CANNOT ASK ANYONE WHERE NARCISSUS IS. SHE CAN ONLY REPEAT WHAT OTHERS SAY.
HELLO, ECHO! NOW WE KNOW YOUR STORY.
...STORY!

MEET THE STARFISH

Script and Illustrations: Pradeep Sathe

CAN YOU SEE A BEAUTIFUL SHAPE ON THAT ROCK? NO, IT IS NOT A FLOWER. IT IS A STARFISH.

A MISLEADING NAME, REALLY. BECAUSE, THOUGH IT MAY LOOK LIKE A STAR, IT IS CERTAINLY NOT A FISH.

A WAVE STRIKES THE ROCK BUT IT CANNOT WASH THE STARFISH AWAY.

THE CREATURE IS HOLDING ON FIRMLY WITH SUCKER TUBES ON THE UNDERSIDE OF ITS ARMS.

ANOTHER WAVE! THIS TIME THE STARFISH LOOSENS ITS GRIP AND THE WAVE CARRIES THE CREATURE INTO THE WATER.

THE STARFISH CAN STAY OUT OF THE WATER AS LONG AS ITS BODY IS MOIST. BUT IT CAN'T BREATHE IN AIR. IT BREATHES IN WATER THROUGH THESE TINY PORES ON ITS BODY.

LET US DIVE AFTER THE STARFISH.

THERE IT IS, LYING ON THE SEA-BED!

OH, IT CAN WALK! IT KEEPS ONE ARM STRAIGHT AND PUSHES ITSELF FORWARD IN THAT DIRECTION WITH THE OTHER FOUR ARMS.

IT HAS CAUGHT A SMALL OYSTER.

IT USES THE SUCKER TUBES ON ITS ARM TO PUSH THE OYSTER UNDER ITS BODY...

...WHERE ITS MOUTH IS SITUATED.

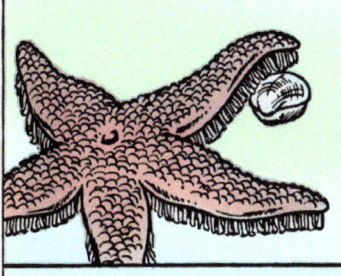

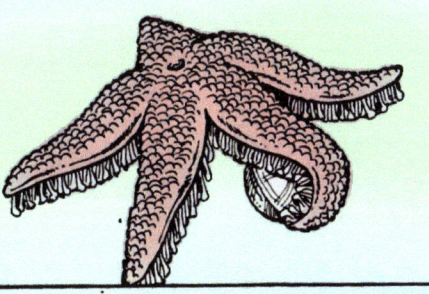

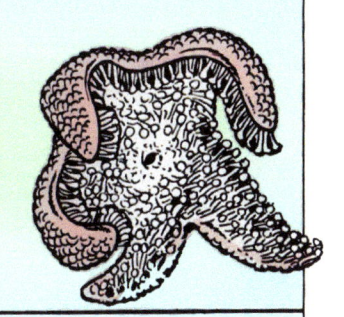

IT PRISES OPEN THE OYSTER WITH ITS MOUTH.

AND SWALLOWS IT WHOLE.

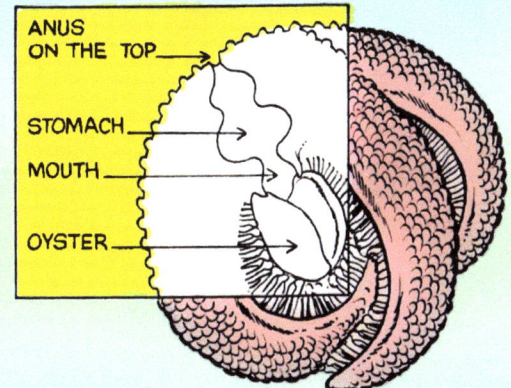

ANUS ON THE TOP
STOMACH
MOUTH
OYSTER

THE MOUTH IS CONNECTED DIRECTLY TO THE STOMACH.

AFTER THE SOFT BODY OF THE OYSTER HAS BEEN DIGESTED THE SHELLS ARE THROWN OUT THROUGH THE MOUTH. AND THE STARFISH WALKS AWAY.

WOW! IT HAS CAUGHT A LARGE OYSTER THIS TIME!

BUT THIS OYSTER IS TOO BIG TO SWALLOW. SO IT TRIES TO OPEN THE OYSTER.

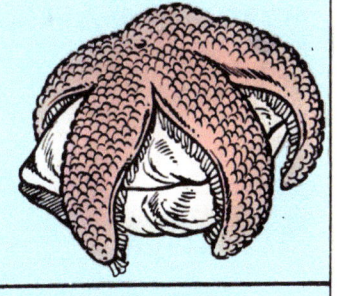

AN HOUR OR TWO LATER THE STARFISH IS ABLE TO FORCE THE SHELLS SLOWLY APART.

THEN AN UNBELIEVABLE THING HAPPENS. THE STARFISH PUSHES ITS STOMACH OUT THROUGH ITS MOUTH AND IN BETWEEN THE OYSTER SHELLS. THE STOMACH POURS DIGESTIVE JUICES ON THE SOFT BODY OF THE OYSTER.

THE OYSTER'S BODY TURNS INTO LIQUID. THE STOMACH ABSORBS THE LIQUID AND THEN GOES BACK INTO THE BODY THROUGH THE MOUTH.
STARFISH EAT CRABS AND OTHER MARINE CREATURES TOO.

MALES AND FEMALES LOOK ALIKE. YOU CAN'T TELL ONE FROM THE OTHER.

— PORES —

IN THEIR BREEDING SEASON, THE MALE HELPS THE FEMALE (BY PRESSING HER BODY) TO LAY EGGS. HERE THEY ARE! THE FEMALE HAS STARTED LAYING EGGS.

THE EGGS COME OUT FROM PORES IN HER ARMPITS. ONE, TWO, THREE, FOUR, FIVE... DON'T TRY TO COUNT THE EGGS...

...BECAUSE THE FEMALE STARFISH LAYS MILLIONS OF EGGS AT A TIME. THE MAXIMUM NUMBER CAN BE 200 MILLION.

WHEN THE EGGS HAVE BEEN LAID THE PARENTS JUST WALK AWAY FROM THEM.

SOME DAYS LATER THE EGGS HATCH AND THE LARVAE COME OUT. THEY SWIM FREELY IN THE WATER.

THEIR SUCKER-TUBES ARE NOT STRONG ENOUGH TO GET A HOLD ON ROCKS OR THE SEABED, YET.

WITHIN A FEW DAYS THE LARVAE GROW THREE ARMS.

FOR ABOUT TWO MONTHS THEY DRIFT WITH PLANKTON (TINY FLOATING CREATURES AND PLANTS OF THE SEA). MEANWHILE, THEY DEVELOP TWO MORE ARMS.

THEN THEY LEAVE THE COMPANY OF THE PLANKTON AND ANCHOR THEMSELVES ON A SOLID SURFACE, LIKE A ROCK OR CORAL...

...AND SLOWLY JOIN THE GROUP OF OTHER STARFISH ON THE SEA-BED.

THE MOST REMARKABLE FEATURE OF THE STARFISH IS ITS ABILITY TO RE-GROW LOST PARTS OF ITS BODY. A STARFISH CAN LOSE ALL ITS ARMS BUT ONE, AND STILL SURVIVE. VERY SOON IT GROWS NEW ARMS.

AN ARM CUT AWAY FROM A STARFISH WILL GROW ANOTHER BODY AND FOUR MORE ARMS.

SO IF YOU CUT A STARFISH INTO FIVE PIECES AND THROW THEM INTO THE SEA, WITHIN A FEW DAYS THERE WILL BE FIVE STARFISHES.

JUST NOW WE'VE MET THE COMMON STARFISH. HERE ARE SOME OTHER STARFISH. ALL OF THEM CAN REGENERATE LOST PARTS OF THEIR BODIES.

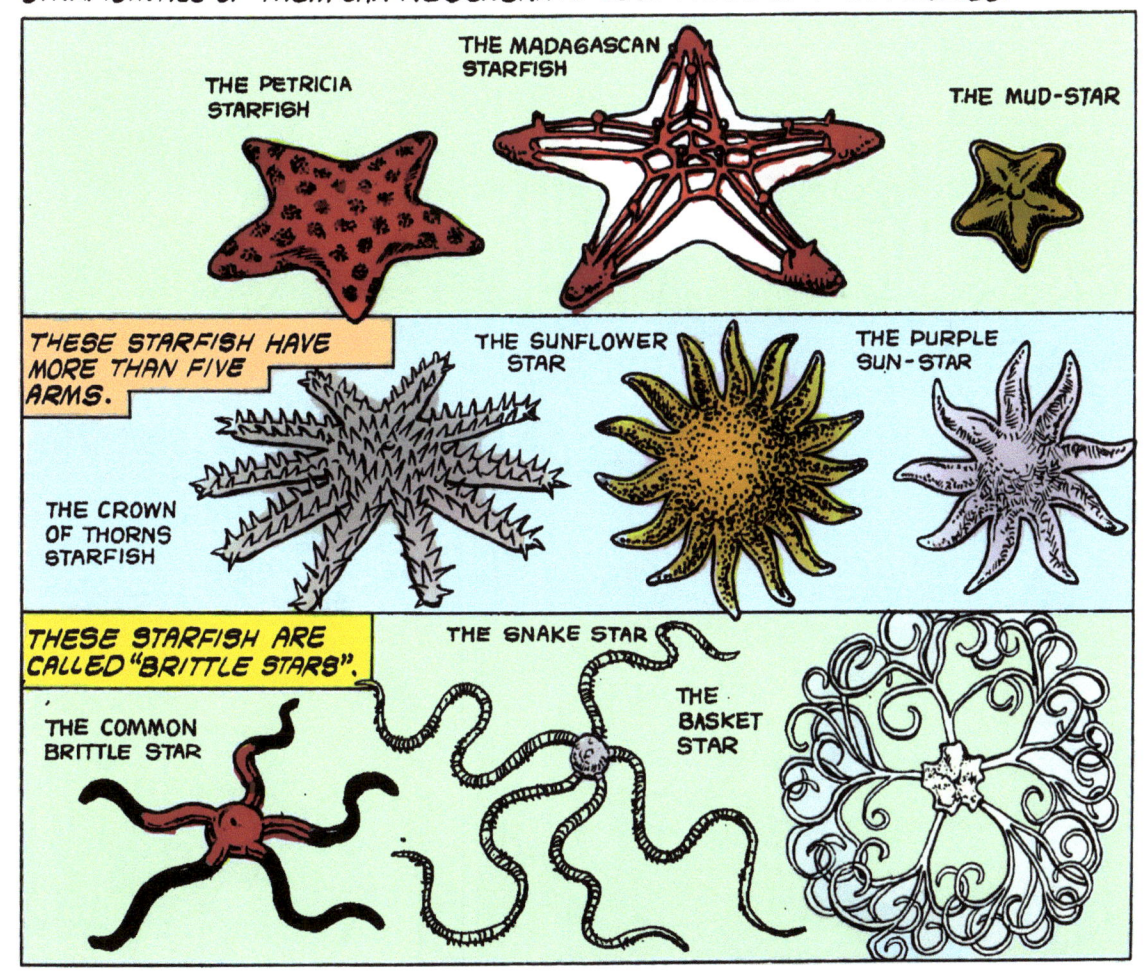

THE PETRICIA STARFISH

THE MADAGASCAN STARFISH

THE MUD-STAR

THESE STARFISH HAVE MORE THAN FIVE ARMS.

THE CROWN OF THORNS STARFISH

THE SUNFLOWER STAR

THE PURPLE SUN-STAR

THESE STARFISH ARE CALLED "BRITTLE STARS".

THE COMMON BRITTLE STAR

THE SNAKE STAR

THE BASKET STAR

FOOLISH BHOLA

Illustrations: V.B. Halbe

Readers' Choice

Based on a story sent by G. Srinivas, Secunderabad

ON THE WAY BACK, BHOLA COULD NOT RESTRAIN HIS CURIOSITY.
DOCTOR, HOW DID YOU KNOW THAT HE HAD EATEN PEANUTS?
IT WAS SIMPLE.
I SAW PEANUT SHELLS ON THE FLOOR.
YOU ARE SO CLEVER.
A FEW DAYS LATER—
WHERE'S THE DOCTOR? MY GRANDSON HAS FEVER.
THE DOCTOR'S NOT IN. BUT I'LL COME INSTEAD.
BHOLA WENT TO SEE HIS VERY FIRST PATIENT, FEELING QUITE IMPORTANT.
MAKE WAY... MAKE WAY FOR THE DOCTOR'S COMPOUNDER. HE HAS COME TO TREAT MY GRANDSON.
THE OTHER PEOPLE GATHERED AROUND TO WATCH. BHOLA FELT QUITE NERVOUS.
HAVE... HAVE YOU EATEN TOO MUCH OF SOMETHING?
WHY, NO!

NOW LET ME LOOK AROUND CAREFULLY...
HMM... NOTHING YOU SAID?
BUT YOU CANNOT HIDE THE TRUTH FROM ME. I KNOW WHAT YOU'VE EATEN.
YOU'VE EATEN A TIGER!
A TIGER!
HAVE YOU COME HERE TO MAKE FUN OF US!
HOW CAN ANYBODY EAT A TIGER, YOU FOOLISH MAN?
I... I...
MAKE WAY, MAKE WAY. THE DOCTOR IS HERE.
SAVED!
FROM NOW ON, I WON'T MAKE ANY MORE HOUSE CALLS!

ANWAR
by
Appaswami
Illustrations: V. B. Halbe
ANWAR, WHAT ARE YOU DOING?
I'M WALKING MY PET, PICHPICHI.
A SNAIL! HA HA HA!
BOW WOW!
YOU SHOULD HAVE A DOG LIKE TIGER!
WHEN I CLAP MY HANDS ...
... HE STANDS ON HIS HEAD!
HE CAN SHAKE HANDS TOO.., CAN PICHPICHI DO ANY TRICKS?
THERE'S ONE THING HE CAN DO THAT YOUR DOG CAN'T!
THAT'S A LAUGH!
TIGER CAN DO ANYTHING YOUR STUPID SNAIL CAN.
PICHPICHI CARRIES HIS HOME ON HIS BACK. LET'S SEE YOUR DOG DO THAT!

Start a subscription and get a brand new Tinkle issue every fortnight!

Get the latest editions of Tinkle delivered straight to your doorstep!

TINKLE MAGAZINE
ANNUAL SUBSCRIPTION
COVER PRICE ₹1200
OFFER PRICE ₹1149
+ Surprise Gift

24 ISSUES

TINKLE COMBO
ANNUAL SUBSCRIPTION
COVER PRICE ₹3120
OFFER PRICE ₹2149
+ Surprise Gift

12 ISSUES

PLEASE ALLOW FOUR TO SIX WEEKS FOR YOUR SUBSCRIPTION TO BEGIN!

OFFER VALID TILL JUNE 30TH 2020

YOUR DETAILS

Full Name: .... Date of Birth: ☐☐ ☐☐ ☐☐☐☐
Address: ....
City: .... State: .... Pin Code: ☐☐☐☐☐☐
Phone/Mobile No.: ☐☐☐ ☐☐☐☐☐☐☐☐
Email: ....

Parent's Signature

PAYMENT OPTIONS

Cheque/DD: ☐☐☐☐☐☐ drawn in favour of 'ACK MEDIA DIRECT LTD.' on bank ....
.... for amount .... Dated: ☐☐ / ☐☐ / ☐☐

SEND US YOUR COMPLETED FORM WITH YOUR CHEQUE/DD AT:
ACK Media Direct Ltd., AFL House, 7th Floor, Lok Bharati Complex, Marol-Maroshi Road, Andheri (East), Mumbai 400 059.

MORE WAYS TO SUBSCRIBE: www.amarchitrakatha.com | customerservice@ack-media.com | +91-22-49188881/2

TIME FOR A
WARDROBE
MAKEOVER!
Choose from Tinkle's brand new range of tee shirts featuring Suppandi and Shambu!
Chef!
I ♥ FRY DAYS
ZZZ YOU LATER, ALLIGATORS!
₹599 ONLY!
01
CHAMPION
Check out our entire catalogue on www.amarchitrakatha.com
Images shown are for representative purposes only.
Actual product may vary.